I0735519

ADVENT

MICHAEL KAMAKANA

PULP LITERATURE PRESS

Library and Archives Canada Cataloguing in Publication

ISBN: 978-1-988865-09-6 (paperback)
ISBN: 978-1-988865-10-2 (ebook)

Cover art: Mel Anastasiou
Cover design: Kate Landels
Interior layout and design: Ellen Michelle

Printed and bound by Ingram/Lightning Source

Published in Canada by Pulp Literature Press
www.pulpliterature.com

For everyone at the house

CONTENTS

ARRIVAL

I go to the pool in the complex every morning for this is not possible in winter in my home city, or even possible in summer for the pool there is in the University and only open to public swimming for certain hours. I go to the pool when the sun is not yet up and the air is cool and the garden and lawn and beach are muted in dawn. I go to swim alone. I am not cold but cool and the pool water is smooth as a mirror without the slightest breeze, and I take off my watch, I take off my sunglasses, and wrap them in the large beach towel that I put beside the chaise longue. I look up to an empty tropical sky. I listen to the wild chickens. I watch the old men who fish off the pier already perched on their chairs. I watch the calm surf hissing and disappearing in the sand. I am about to step into the pool when my father calls down to me from the lanai. I look up and for a moment fear captures my thoughts, for he is deliberately calm as he ever is in a serious moment, but then my mother appears beside him and I do not fear. I know my parents are reaching that age when death is said to be of natural causes, but to me that nature is difficult to imagine. I wonder what they are watching at this time on the television that I hear. I remember the cold war terror I had felt as a child one vacation when the air raid siren went off, when I thought of the air force base nearby, but no one seemed to care, no one moved faster, no one even noticed, and my mother saw how upset I was and told me it was only a test they run every first Monday of each month. I remember that terror and it seems to join this as I hear other televisions come on and voices raised and the sudden quiet murmur of many electrical vehicles starting. I move more quickly and wonder what has happened for this is midday on the Eastern Seaboard and news is often keyed to that time zone. I come up to the condo where Mom is held closely to my father but he glances to me and then to the flatscreen. I turn to the images as they lower the volume, but I can hear the televisions from all the other condos and this does not clarify what has happened. I watch the explosion of a crashing airplane but this is not into buildings in New York. I watch a honking gridlock of red brake lights. I watch buildings on fire. I watch subways immobile. I watch surging groups of people who have swarmed on urban streets, some waving flags and banners, some dancing, some fighting, some embracing, some raising their phones to record images, some standing alone. I watch quickly rendered computer graphics that point to various locations around the world, some at midnight, some at midday, some at dawn, some at dusk, but everywhere with too many faces staring and babbling in their local language, with scrolled translations, with a clock that is somehow hours past and not current. This news came in the night to most of the cities of the mainland, but there is now an explanation why we are hearing this only now. Power down, the terrified face claims. All the power was down. Father looks to me and takes a deep breath. Mom holds on more tightly to him.

RESET

When the aliens came it was not what we expected. We did not even realize that human history had come to an end. We wanted to believe that the aliens were just a new aspect of our human world. We wanted to believe that whatever was to happen we humans were the central protagonists. We were shocked but quickly adjusted to this advent, even as we necessarily saw it as a radical change in our human story with unsuspected new characters. In our sense of history the aliens were long expected. We wondered how anyone could have ever imagined persisting secrecy, could have ever imagined this advent would not change everything in our human story. We could think in terms of narratives. We could imagine what we could not before imagine. We were ready for this adventure. We had seen the movies. We were ready to reset or adjust to this new feature of our human lives. We thought that somehow we would continue, that no matter how the aliens were disposed to us, we adaptable humans would find common qualities, find logic, find love, find hatred, find some meaning to this encounter. We were proud, we were fearful, we were tentative, we thought ourselves at the beginning of a wondrous new history and not simply at the end of human history. Some people were happily amazed, though this reaction did not long persist. Some people were immediately fearful. Some people were joyous. Some people were in dislocating shock and unable to react either way. Some people were ecstatic to be visited by elder beings of another evolution that knew so many, many, magical technologies. We had in those first days, first months, first years, many and often conflicting ideas of what did they want, what did we want, what did this all mean. Some people saw the aliens as aliens. Some people who were religious claimed these aliens were actually gods or emissaries or potentates or facilitators of their god or gods. Some people who were atheists claimed this was proof that the universe, if not the world, was a natural creation. Some people lost their faith, some people gained a new faith. Some people tried to form a religion around the aliens but there was nothing we could call miracle, judgment, grace, damnation — in fact, nothing humans had previously called religious. Some people said we defined religious experience, religious sentiment, too narrowly and typically in our postindustrial way. Some people said we were lucky to see the inevitable triumph of the true spiritual world, the true church, the last church. Some people saw great promise in the aliens, some great fear. Our merely human leaders could only hold their breath, hold it long and longer, until finally collapsing with piercing mental anguish. Some people lost their minds and acted out their madness. Some people insisted they were now possessed by these aliens, excusing fantastic and horrific crimes, revealing by their acts just how alien were these others. We were all human now, truly. We were ready to discover just how human we all were and what that status meant. We were human, but no one knew that when the aliens came our proud claims, our human insistence, our human naming was no longer ours to make. We humans perhaps all wanted the same things, food for our families, shelter from the rain or snow or burning sun and scouring sandstorms, care for our elders, a future for our children. We simply have fatal disagreements on how our desires are needs, how desires are ordered in importance — as spiritually deferred or materially immediate — how we can best satisfy our needs. But such conflicts have always been so before the aliens came and was not so different now. We saw that the impoverished subcontinental weavers of our shirts, our trousers, our suits and dresses, were as human as those of us in the postindustrial world of hedge funds, of insurance, of banking in all its varied forms, who never previously thought of those who died in buildings that collapsed from overloaded floors in ravaging fire and suffocating smoke behind locked fire escapes, or those simply poisoned by the rare metals factories webbed into our innumerable phones and other electronics. We were all human, now. We suspended capital, denied debts and loans, struggled to imagine what the aliens used as matrices for their obviously highly technological society. Some people thought their intervention in our world was proof that capitalism or socialism, that technocracy or theocracy, as practised here or there in lamentably human imperfection, was the answer to how we humans should live. Some people believed that through enlightened reverse engineering we would be able to leap into a future in which there would be no distinction between magic and technology. Some people believed all our typical human problems were soon to be solved. Some people thought this meant that we would now become men like gods. Some people were certain it would only be their like-minded cohorts of religion, of wealth, of skin colour, of nose size, of eye shape who would be selected to gain from untold alien benefits. Some people fled the cities to hide in caves or farms or extensive plantations or private islands or untracked wilderness. Some people abandoned their farms and came to the cities. Some people fanatically insisted on continuing to live no differently than they had before the advent. Some people fatalistically refused to live anything like the way they did before. Some people circulated conspiracy theories.

Some people said the aliens were not aliens but actually this or that usual scapegoat, maybe Jewish or maybe Muslim or maybe American. Some people said the aliens were actually artificial intelligence or time travellers or persistent mass hallucinations or a glitch in that endless computer simulation of our human lives. We were wrong.

REAL

He is a man who knows the joy of finding things out. He is a man who was a boy who knew the joy of finding things out. He is a man who has discovered a place where finding things out is approved, a place where it is rewarded, a place where it is central to his entire working project. This is what he discovered after one university class on physics while he was studying as an engineering major. He is a man who was a boy who only knew of practical occupation for his skills with math and science, knew only of the profession of engineer, knew only of design and building by engineering in a mechanical sense. He is a man who learns about chemical engineering after mechanical engineering, who learns there is another way to use his intellectual aptitude, learns there is something so perfectly abstract in finding things out, learns of university professors, learns that this career leads to use and freedom and secure employment, learns by studying in one undergraduate class about physics as required by the engineering faculty for graduation. He walks across the quad, autumn leaves orange and gold skittering in the crisp breeze, crackling under his step, swirling against stone steps before this university building entrance gathering all the falling leaves, but no one stops to notice this, he least of all. He is not here. He is thinking about the innovation of Boyle's law of ideal gas, how the higher the density, the higher the energy, the faster and stronger the energy released in expansion. He knows that for a fixed amount of an ideal gas kept at a fixed temperature, pressure and volume are inversely proportional. He is thinking he has known this in a practical way, known this is the essential gaseous energy transformed into mechanical energy, known this is the principle by which all automotive and other internal combustion engines work. He has known this but he has not known this. He is thinking about how this has been known but not how he has known, for though he never imagined it was magic that powered such engines, he has usually imagined only the obvious working parts, parts like combustion chambers, like spark plugs, like pistons, like crankshafts, like exhaust. He could see them in action, he could understand how engineers would try to improve each generation of automobile, even how such engines powered small aircraft propellers, even how this model of engine was surpassed by turbines, by jets, by rockets. But whatever form it was always Boyle's law that was applied. He is thinking of this with each distracted step, his brow furrowed as if in pain but truly only in concentration. He is thinking of this wondrous theoretical discovery, but not of the man or men or the details of how this was discovered. Only the elegance, the beauty, the power, of that theory. He is not able to say at which step on the playful leaves he comes to understand he must leave the engineering faculty where he is on scholarship and switch his major to physics. He is not able then, or later, to recall the moment of this decision. He does not know the time of day nor the day of the week, but he does recall the term and from this the year and maybe it clarifies in his mind much later, decades later, when he finds a solid block of books with sketches and math and symbols which speak of this physics class which convinced him of what he must do. He finds these lecture notes in an old cardboard box by his desk at home, and some kind of pleasure comes back, some memory, some joy, some surprise, all emotions, for he had long forgotten how very good were these notes. He is walking across the quad, he is mounting the steps, he is wearing a cracked black leather jacket, rough blue jeans, he is thinking with a scowl that only adds to his unapproachable presence. He frightens one student who immediately steps aside wondering what this hoodlum is doing entering the physics building rather than, probably, racking up some billiard table in a basement downtown. He is not even aware of this student. He is not here. He is walking now on black-speckled gray linoleum scuffed with a history of so many footprints, wood panels dark brown halfway up the walls, closed frosted-glass and wood doors into lecture halls, panels open above the doors, muted lectures, solid polite silence, but he is walking past these chambers and to the office. Later, he will never able to recall exactly to whom or how he had spoken or even if they had tried to dissuade him. He might have been momentarily worried about money but probably not. He has grown up rural poor. He knows grinding poverty but is confident he will never allow this to happen to him. He speaks softly to the secretary to set an appointment, and despite his surly appearance, despite his lack of academic pose, despite all this he seems polite enough. He is confident but he is not confident. He briefly allows his anxiety to surface when the woman gives him necessary application papers and points to where he needs to sign, where he needs this man to sign, where he needs this other man to sign. He has not thought that this action will be denied, has not for a moment imagined alternatives, has not for a moment conceived arguments or assertions that will make this change real in his world and not the worlds of hopes and dreams. He does so now. His eyes blur, his body shivers unseen, as he thinks about how there must finally be some reason to be turned away, some reason the university will not allow him to major in physics, some reason he cannot anticipate and he cannot overcome. He does not remember discussing this change of major here at the office or ever before to his roommates, all fellow students as well in the process of dispersing from engineering to other majors, such that of the four none will actually become an engineer. He does not realize that it is his example, his certainty, his leadership unspoken that allows them one after another to switch to chemistry, to physics, to physical chemistry, to chemical physics. He does not realize that what he does with such confidence allows the other three young men to each question their own paths. He has an unspoken and unsolicited effect such that when questions arise, questions of any sort, even of what beer to drink or what pizza to order, he will listen to relevant arguments and positions then with a dismissive shrug will ignore the others and do whatever he originally wanted. He has always been the unifying force for any projects with his friends because he is imaginative but knows when to halt thoughts and just do, never focusing on what might happen but only on what he wants to do. He is dedicated and serious and focused when he has set a goal. He knows his goal is to never become his father. He has seen his father, after years of independence as a silver fox farmer, after years surviving the blight of the Great Depression, after years with no other futures awaiting or possible, become the night watchman at the town foundry. His father has to be servile at most, has to be modest at least, has to be glad that even this minor employment was there for it enables him to keep the family farm and see off his son to university. His father is trapped by his own conscience and the son knows well enough that he would suffer the same if he had made commitments, if he was married, if he had children, if he had hopes for their future. He knows well enough this would become if not a welcome burden of responsibility, an adult load of responsibility, an adult life. He has never had illusions that the world was a welcoming place, he knew that he needed to

wrest his future from denying forces, from poverty, from children, from the fox farm. He would never suffer the injustice of
working for a living, having a boss, having limits, having to
answer Sir, having to rely only on skills any healthy man might
own. He will never be his father. He is thinking thoughts like
this often when he thinks of his future but it may be an error to
call these thoughts, as certainly they are not conscious preoccu-
pations, as he cannot remember ever voicing this fear aloud or
allowing it to hinder his accomplishments, as he must have come
to this attitude from his youngest years, from his youth, his
adolescence, his long wanderings in the bush when hunting was
only an excuse to leave home, leave the farm, leave the emotional
turmoil of his sisters and his mother and his father. He does not
think these thoughts. He set this goal when he was young, when
he first saw the world was not good enough for his father. His
father had also once hunted and trapped and seemed headed for
a life as woodsman, as bachelor, as town eccentric, when he met
this cousin who came from her own family farm to the north,
this woman whose fierce intelligence and uncompromising ideals
had frightened off other men who saw only her raven hair and
blue eyes, this woman already older than the usual marrying
age, he met her, he loved her, he married her. He was not afraid
of her intelligence but rather attracted to it, for in some ways it
validated his own intelligence, his unschooled autodidactic
knowledge from however many years he had not attended the
distant high school because his family could not afford it, from
these years of all the books he read, books he hid from the jeers
of fellows who saw no wisdom and no value in packets of open
pages. He was not afraid of her intelligence, he was not afraid of
her years, he was not afraid of becoming a father, of shouldering
the load of any man, of the sincere promise to try to make her
happy or at least glad to have married him. His father could not
know what tragedy awaited this beautiful and lively and so very

smart woman. He himself had never known his mother before her illness. His elder sister had. His father had. He is thinking these thoughts as he gazes at the papers the secretary proffers, but he is not thinking these thoughts, these thoughts are buried, ignored, and the important thing is to find out how things work, how to do this and do that if he truly wishes to shift his major. He looks at this kindly secretary, this woman so old she must be someone's mother, someone he goes to classes with, maybe a young woman, maybe a young man, and without consciously recognizing this urge he finds he wants to please this stranger. He looks like one of those movie juvenile delinquents but at the moment wishes he were not wearing the aviator leather jacket, this costume that had only this morning satisfied his aggressive mood. He wants to now be wearing a suit, something right for this meeting, something that would announce his serious intent, his studious intent, his true desire to become one of those professors with whom this secretary must work. He hears the regular clatter of typewriting. He hears voices but not words, voices calm, voices measured, voices overlapped, voices start and go or question and response behind another frosted-glass door, but it is the secretary who collects his awareness when she notes it is here on this page and here on this other page he must note his current class marks, that there is a threshold he must pass, and at the thought of this simple barrier he feels the twitching of a coming smile. He knows his marks are good enough, they always have been, but here is the pleasure of finding things out, here is the world invisible but unavoidable, here is some definition of this project, here is something he can do. He hears the secretary ask if he wishes to speak to a counsellor but this only allows him to smile truly. He is a man who knows the joy of finding things out. He is smiling because now he knows how this will work. He sees a responding empathic smile rising on the secretary's face, rising but not full for she does not know whether he is smiling in confident dismissal of this problem or wry acceptance of an insurmountable barrier. He is aware of the entire admissions office this present moment in the way it is said women remember the dress they were wearing when they met the man they would marry. He is aware of the enamel off-white walls, the dark wood wainscoting, the dark wooden secretary desks, the dark wooden counter on which the papers are arrayed, the green carpet flattened by traffic here and covered by plastic mats there under wheeled swivelling chairs, the quiet when the voices stop and there is a pause in the typing, he is aware of all this, this world, this moment, but later, years later, decades later, he will claim he has no memories of this place even when jolted to memory by finding those physics notes. He finds this block of notes as if he had been wrapping them for transport but for whom and for where he does not recall, and though he does not allow travel in mind to his youth, to his university years, to when he had not accomplished his many goals yet and there were only unknowable reasons and emotional anxiety that he might fail. He will not remember the time of day, the day of the week, only that it must have been after midterm exam marks had been posted. He has seen his marks for physics and maybe this is the moment he decides to become a physicist. He is a man who knows the joy of finding things out and today he has found out what he wants to do. He looks down to the forms, the tinted green area not for him but for the office, then in black the lines, the boxes, the small print here, the smaller print there, the areas he must fill out, how here he must find the scholarship people or the counsellor or this or that professor to sign. He is never intimidated by administration forms, not here as a student, not decades later as a professor, for someone has logically predetermined what they need to know and how and from whom and often there are even notices of deadlines, there are arrows directing the applicant, there are boxes and lines where he must sign. He is not intimidated. He is not uncertain. He can tell there is someone who has logically thought out what information must be given. He is pleased. He can find things out. He is comfortable because no one is asking irrelevant questions or demanding emotional appeals and no one on this paper demands to know why he is switching majors. He finds this lack of question respects his freedom, in itself this question is so confident that perhaps the true question should be why he would ever have had this previous major, how could he ever have wanted to be only an engineer when he could be a physicist. He looks at the papers. He looks up to the secretary. He recognizes an expectant face, realizes she has asked a question and awaits an answer, and for a moment he tenses up and his smile falls to confusion. He is for only the briefest fraction of a second abandoned or expelled by this world where everything makes sense, and it is the worlds left behind that threaten to engulf him again, to capture him, to deny him escape. He suddenly loses all confidence and his face is one of naked appeal, of imminent hurt, of childhood appeal, of horror and fear that he will be rejected. He will look this way that only several decades later and only without thought, when he will be faced with the death of his son, death that truly cannot be known, but here and now this look is only a passing moment he over-comes, and the secretary who asks the question does not press the enquiry but incorporates this into a new question so that he need not ask her again. He is grateful for her tact. He looks at her and for a moment imagines her as his mother. He knows she is someone's mother. He smiles and wonders if this is a sufficient gesture of gratitude, wonders if there is pity, or simple comfort, behind her pleasant gaze. He allows such internal questions to lapse almost as he asks them, for this is the terrain of emotions, and becoming emotional has always seemed to him frivolous and irrelevant and something to avoid at all costs. He does not recognize that it is emotions that are leading him to switch majors, or at least that they are a minor component easily submerged in all the rational arguments he would form if anyone asked him. He would listen. He would dismiss. He would do what he has always wanted. He looks down at the paper, ashamed at revealing his emotions even in that passing look, but the secretary is kindly and does not even mention this. He sees his reflection for a moment in her glasses but he seems far away and perhaps such a glimpse was imaginary, and anyway how could light, just light, describe what is seen for light is itself invisible wavelengths but for lasers, light is nothing more than that which it illuminates. These are not even thoughts now, though years later he collects his lecture notes and they are published as his textbook introduction to quantum concepts in spectroscopy, and this is the study of light, but of course at this moment it is as irrelevant as anything emotional. He looks at this secretary who now seems inordinately patient and kind and for a moment he wonders if he has missed another question or whether she is about to ask him another or if he should ask a question or if she has answered a question he does not remember asking. He is not thinking on any accessible level but only feeling from cores of self he usually refuses to visit. He is feeling grateful and happy that this is a secretary, a function, a role, someone who exists in a concrete and logical position to help him figure things out, here, now, finding things out to transfer majors, finding things out to talk to scholarship people, finding things out to do this and how to do that thing, to fill out these papers, to have them signed, then deliver them here, to wait, to receive, for though there is always a gap between application and response he will have done everything that can be done. He looks at the abstract, the logical, and the sensible papers and is pleased he will do this without arguing with another, without justifying, without politics, above all without emotion. He nods to the secretary and in a moment will leave. He will in memory have no sense of the importance of this moment, this decisive, this indicative moment that can only be called emotional later, years later, decades later, if only he could remember it. He knows that at the moment he does not know this. He feels the tremor of his doubt pass unremembered, and maybe another student's mind would be distracted by other more reasonable concerns, by how he will pass the weekend, how he will finally talk to this girl at the library, just a girl, just another ordinary university student who works there, who smiles when gathering other books from the table at which he works, who asks him if he is reading these other books and the answer is always no. He could think of this and renew his resolution to whisper with her, he could be an ordinary young man, he could be one of the other university students but none of this is the case. He could be an ordinary student, or so he thinks later, years later, but that he does not allow emotional distraction is more consistent with who he was and who he is. He is not thinking of the future in this ordinary way, he is thinking of the future path, the future classes, the future focus, thoughts gathering on his brow with such intensity the secretary at the counter worries that she has not been clear, or that he is confused or angry about something she has not said, something that threatens his plan to switch majors from engineering to physics. He is not thinking these thoughts. He is only momentarily cast back to the time he crossed the quad thinking about Boyle's law no more than half an hour before, but he had already discarded those other real concerns, those ordinary concerns, those social anxieties, because the scattering fallen leaves of orange and gold had not obscured the dark wet grey of the concrete sidewalk, something that made sense and denoted how things worked, somebody recognized the walk should go here, should lead from point (a) to point (b) by the shortest route. He was wearing work clothes that were young and angry, and he had felt pleased only that morning to look like a delinquent, to look threatening, then he had come to the university and for a moment wished he was in a suit, a sport jacket, a vest, a lettered sweater, something, but now he feels confident again. He is finding things out. He has begun the necessary actions to switch his major from engineering to physics. He is not his costume, he is not his surly look, he is nothing but the young man who will fill out these forms, just a series of questions answered, just boxes filled in and lines signed, just exactly what he has wanted to be. He might have wanted to be that actor in his breakthrough role who has just died in a car crash, who all the sillier young women and probably his younger sister, if not his elder sister, had launched into celebrity mourning. He might have wanted to be the focus for such outpourings of emotion, but he has seen the movie and found it difficult to sympathize with the young suburban Hollywood teen, with any of the teens, the rebels who had no cause to rebel. He might have wanted to be this way but he will later smile, years later, decades later, to identify him with those teens. He is not sympathetic to either those teens or himself. He does not remember how he had wanted a red jacket, how he had wanted wavy hair, how he had wanted to somehow emulate or at least suggest that character. He does not remember this as he does not remember many things that are finally irrelevant and emotional, if everything that is emotional is not by definition irrelevant. He thinks of this intuitive equation he must have discovered when he was very young, when he had first learned that emotions were not things to find out but things to avoid. He had fled home immediately after finishing chores, before new charges might be ordered, had fled to the world of imagination and knowledge that even left behind his usual companion younger sister. He had fled in later years, in adolescence, because his mother was yet more ill and would never be better, his mother who had demanded him as a child to prove he loved her. He had been a child. He could never satisfy this demand. He will know later, years later, decades later, that this had been an emotional demand that pretended to surpass all rational determination, but he could not know and could not voice this as a child. He had seen this demand accepted and suffered then by his father. His sisters had been likewise emotional and for the elder, who had known their mother before the decline of her health, her raven hair, her blue eyes, her lively, fierce intelligence, this would remain on the surface and in the core of all the memories, so he had decided to forget. He had of course identified with his father, and later, years later, decades later, forgiven his father for the long affair he had courted with another woman just down the road. He has forgiven that which he no longer forgets. He does not finally forget his mother but he does not forget how he had loved his mother, how this love was never enough, how this love was a deficit, an intractable problem, a problem he cannot this moment translate into logical terms, into finely measured thoughts, but only into emotional terrain he will not now, will not ever, believe he can surpass or overcome. He can only avoid at this moment. He remembers what vulgar Freudianism claimed that somehow, without conscious thought, he the boy would want to have sex with his mother, he the boy would fear castration from his father, he knows these assertions go this way, claim to see him this way, and insist this absurd claim was somehow key to too many other aspects of his conscious life. How absurd, how grotesque, how mistaken this original psychological insight is, he thinks of those other students, students he does not know, students in those social sciences which have no actual science, real science, science he knows, theoretical science such as the discovery of Boyle's law, theoretical science which underpins practical science, applicable science, and through this engineering and the real world. He thinks of his sisters elder and younger who probably know the advanced arguments of psychiatry, but if it comes to this assertion of emotional, unconscious desires and fears, he is not interested, he is at the start repulsed, he will not read on any more than he does if the book he is reading comes to an absurd or painful end, he will just not read on, and anyway if this is a claim for the unconscious that is where it should stay. He does not see how the only answer is to allow his conscious mind to control this meaningless, heaving, shapeless ocean of the unconscious. He is thinking these thoughts, though maybe it is wrong to honour them with the term thoughts, though these precede and are overcome by his conscious thoughts. He tells himself consciously that he is here for a reason, that he knows the joy of finding things out. He looks at the kindly face of the secretary at the admissions office and asks himself how he can prove he loves his mother, and the only answer is here and now, the answer is that he will switch from engineering to physics, the answer is that he will act on some emotional level and escape the logical dispassion of doing what everyone else says is the right thing, escape to what he rightly desires. He does not think these thoughts, not consciously, but he is finding things out. He will later, years later, decades later, admit that he must have been senselessly confident, that maybe he just did not know what could go wrong with his desires, that maybe he took comfort that, whatever path he chose, none would lead to rural poverty, to an educated and intellectual existence among the desperately poor, though of course he will argue that everyone was poor in the Great Depression and through the war and sometimes after, that they were only poor relative to those Hollywood teenagers. He is not thinking these thoughts, he is thinking for some reason of his mother, he is not worrying. He has seen the decline of his mother, he has seen what this sorrow did to his younger sister who was at home, what had drawn his elder sister home in these final days. He sees this but he is helpless, he remains at university and tries not to think of her health. He does not know yet that she will not get better, he does not know that the last time he saw her was the last time he will ever see her. He is a young man who enjoys finding things out. He will go to California sooner than he expects to do his master's in physics at Caltech, but he is not thinking of that yet, he is finding things out, fixing his attention on the lines, the boxes, the green-tinted sections on the application to switch his major from engineering to physics. He is standing equally on his right foot and his left foot, balanced and secure, he is rigid and strong, not brittle or weak, and he could respond quickly to move to his right or move to his left. He is aware on some heightened level, tense and alert even as he is not there, as he is thinking of Boyle's gas law which stimulates him to think of the other laws, the laws he does not yet know that fit securely as puzzle pieces with those laws he has long been familiar with but only in the abstract. He feels joy at how deduction can proceed correctly through these laws, joy that not many will perceive in the same way, not many will be astonished and pleased with all these theories that become laws and axioms, but this is not a joy he can share, not with his sisters elder or younger, not with his father, not with his mother. He knows laws in physics are laws without lawgivers or prosecutors or any kind of legal apparatus, laws absolute and clear and inflexible, laws he will discover in the joy of finding things out. He will claim later, years later, decades later, that he is not inordinately skilled in math, but this is only in comparison to those professors and scientists who are skilled, who can imagine, can judge, can agree, or can disagree. He works with scientists and offers his mind to the others, his mind in which he finds things out, his mind that works with their minds on various themes throughout his career as a scientist. He will recognize that his mind is just not as sharp in math, in the way perhaps athletes can see and judge other athletes or measure skills on some shared basis of time or distance or height or weight, but perhaps he is not realizing how sharp, how shared, how versatile is his mind, for he works with a wide range of fellow scientists, works on quantum concepts of spectroscopy, works on liquid crystal dynamics, works on flow through porous media, works on non-linear dynamics, and he knows or learns enough of each language to interact with the others. He works on understanding each concept well enough to satisfy motivating curiosity, enough for usually seven years, enough to move on to understand another concept. He thinks of himself as a perpetual beginner yet his skill is not in religion or pure abstractions of philosophy but in the physics and math required to satisfy his curiosity. He will know the scientific innovation developed through decades of his career from student to professor has been the increasing power and facility and use of computers. He knows this is seen most clearly in non-linear dynamics, when he first faces this science that can describe apparent chaos as non-linear, this science of living systems. He knows that living chaos can only be calculated with an infinite precision of initial conditions and this results in a recognition that this calculation has no more than statistical validity. He is proud to be a perpetual beginner. He is not ever so religious, but from such a perspective he would be recognized as an eager novice as he switches from engineering and his thoughts determine that there is this original joy of finding things out, that there is a joy he must never lose, there is a joy that is at the moment his secret, his secret alone, though his future colleagues, his under-graduate students, his graduate students, his post-doctorates and associate profs may share each their version of such pleasure. He will elevate and engage his students for this pleasure never does leave, not later, years later, decades later, but they can hear in his lectures or watch in his meetings with them, can sense how this original joy of finding things out is contagious, is never diminished, is what serves him as a good teacher. He is not inordinately skilled with math, but he does know math, he does talk in math to these colleagues, these students, in this logical and rational and precise and unemotional system, this perfectly descriptive language, this language to describe his questions and his answers, this language that takes in theories and responds so correctly to evidence or conflict or what the other has to say. He is not an experimentalist who builds from evidence given, no matter how strange evidence experimentation may give, no matter how he might not know details of the apparatus. None of these factors will matter to him for he is a theoretician and the tools of his trade are papers and pens, chalk and blackboard, computers personal and mainframe, and whatever that process that occurs in his mind and the minds of other colleagues here or on the other side of the world. He is not a mathematician. He does use math and sees some beauty in math as any language that offers the beauty of poetry. He does not question this language that of course preceded him, this language that he feels somehow was the first, the silent, the perfect language that he feels he must have realized from the first operation learned as a child. He did not know why, then. He does not question, now. He knows even as he stands at the admissions counter in the physics building, knows this language completely, beautiful but ineffable and unutterable in any other terms. He knows but he does not know. He knows here is a world where everything makes sense even if it is based on infinite mystery. He knows the beauty of math. He knows acceleration will always be speed over time. He knows the square of a hypotenuse will always equal the sum of the squares of the two other sides of a right triangle, and he can use the ratios sine and cosine to find those lengths of any other triangle, or if the angle is known he can find out the length of the other side, or if the angle is unknown he can discover it from the lengths of these lines. He knows these equations will never change. He knows there are no emotional appeals, no emotions at all, and everything makes sense, and this is what must have started him to this path of becoming a physicist. He sees his sisters elder and younger, he sees his father, he sees his mother, he sees them but he does not see them. He is there but he is not there. He has walked without seeing anyone else, for no one will approach this young man, scowling in his concentration, following his gaze to no distance another may see, walking, deliberate and distracted. He is standing by the telephone downstairs at the house whose rent he shares with three other students, fingering a torn piece of lined paper, folding it as he reads it, puzzled but not worried, then dialling the number of his elder sister. He is surprised at how quickly she answers. He hears the connection made and his elder sister's voice is clear. He waits for her to speak after he identifies himself, there is a pause, a long pause, and possibly a heavy breath. He nods to one of his roommates who, rather than present as the clean-shaven engineering student, has decided to grow the beard and longer hair of that poet of whom even he has heard. He waits on the phone and almost thinks they are cut off, almost asks if she is still there, a shrug to his roommate, but finally she does speak. He takes a breath, he thanks her, he says he understands, he says he will be home this weekend, he hangs up, and he leans against the wall. His roommate looks at him, his roommate a dedicated Catholic who more than once has tried to bring him to Mass, but there are no words now, nothing to say, only unknowing sadness from the inquisitive gaze of his roommate.

RESERVE

When they first came to be on the Reserve it did not seem too different from the way they had always lived. They did not see the walls, did not sense the disconnection, did not at first realize how total would be the information quarantine for which they had opted. They had trusted their democratically elected leaders, though these might have won by appeals to those human religious or cultural prejudices if not simple fear of the others, the humans, the aliens, the humans impatiently becoming the aliens. They had withdrawn from the advent and would try to live as their parents and grandparents had lived, though there were no wars, no plagues, no disruptions of any kind that might winnow the population. They had instead at first a burgeoning population, but for some reason, of the growing children, not many were intending to become parents, and more than a few left the Reserve for the mysterious wonders of the Cities, any cities, which were of course places of fantasy, of magic, of rumour that only secretively propagated the more those elders tried to censor any knowledge. They wanted their children to be truly human. They wanted them not to be corrupted. They did not believe curiosity of the unknown was one of the defining characteristics of children, that children by nature want to know, that it is only mistaken pedagogical models which prohibit such natural learning. They who stayed on the Reserve were perversely against learning, against adapting, even as adults. They were instead conservative and in voting triumphant, but they were not all, many left or were exiled or rejected. On the Reserve there were many human ways to encourage the minority to leave, from bribery to shunning to bullying to trolling, in person or on the radically curtailed Reserve Internet. Some few who remained became like any virus in the corporate body of those who claimed to be True Humans, whose simple presence disrupted their pure ideology, some few who had refused to leave for the Cities because this was their home and had been for generations. Some people did not agree with the voting majority but this did not mean they were convinced to become almost aliens, to become City and world dwellers. Some people had to adjust, every day it seemed, to the waves of alien rejection that one week would erupt in a conspiracy theory that Reserve children television shows were secretly fuelling City propaganda, the next week that far-seeing news was underestimating and thus undermining the growth of True Humans and the number of reserves following their brand of conservatism. Some people had already given up the birthright fight to be True Human, but they were a minority on this Reserve, and their friends had fallen to the lowest social strata in the City to which they had so eagerly fled. They had even sent a few of the righteous to the Cities to investigate how those who had left the Reserve had found it a place of human degradation, a place where all the humans were becoming as like the aliens as possible, not merely painting themselves but speaking the alien way, thinking the alien thoughts, living the alien ways. They maintained that those investigators had not returned to the Reserve because other humans already damned in their false way of living had in some unspecified way corrupted or captured or even killed them. They made appeals to the Reserve Agent, who simply filed it and forgot it. They were told so many young people came to the City, some who had fled the Reserve, some who had even claimed to be investigators or groups of True Humans, who disappeared there, who decided to escape there, who had deliberately moved to the Cities in the only way they could evade the rules and limits of their parents or others, who even if found might refuse to return, and after all, even as children to the Reserve they were responsible for themselves as any humans were to the aliens. They received no help from the Reserve Agent, as human as he might be, and of course the rare alien who met him in the equivalent of flesh, who came perhaps as a sort of tourist to the Reserve, was not even talked to by the True Humans. They were told many times and certainly believed that the real power here was vested in the alien and not its face in the Agent, but even the simplest conversation with one alien was with all aliens, and who knows what the aliens would hear of your private thoughts, your secret thoughts. They were afraid of the aliens and what to a human might be a thought to be disavowed, an urge to be denied, a shameful desire, was to the aliens only meaningless and ineffective human mind babbling. They were afraid the aliens would broadcast what they had heard in their magic way, and while this would not disconcert the aliens, it could disrupt or end any political future amongst your fellow humans, your fellows who might have usual human emotions, might have ordinary hatred, ordinary ignorance, ordinary delusion, but this was yet not something to share with your voters or fellows or families. They might have lusts and desires that the Cities might enable and therefore must be more stridently rejected. They might have perverse intentions to the actual and physical reality of other humans. For the aliens did not magically alleviate the tragic constant of the horrors humans inflict on humans, and nobody could yet ever explain that the pleasure was always power over the reality and not the simulation. They might, in the worst case, be revealed as desiring in their deepest psyche that which they disavowed, desiring the Cities, desiring the aliens. They feared this discovery as much as any phobic would desire their fear. They might escape the condemnation of other True Humans, but never themselves.

RESET

When the aliens came it was not who we expected, but we did not know who to expect, we could not imagine or truly expect the unexpected, the unimaginable. Through our culture and our technology, our intelligence and capabilities, we had for some eras of human history, no longer than an eye blink, had for centuries, had for many lifetimes, dominated our world to such an extent that we felt no qualifiers needed to identify ourselves. We were truly only part of the world but thought ourselves the entire world. We would claim to be the voices of all humans, the voices incorporating all sense, speaking for all our many humans, though there were many humans who would dispute our primacy. We who lost the right to claim such, as became clearer after the aliens came, maintained that we were humans, all too human, but this did not excuse our inhumane history. We were accused by some as the people who had drained resources of the world, who had ruled by market and austerity, who had ruled by sanction and war, who had lived beyond our own means and so had used the means of all other humans. We would later defensively claim it was only a small number of our people who so dominated us as well as these unfortunate others, but these others would reply, if so why did we not stop them, how could we proclaim innocence. If so, when they had so acted, how did they mean it if not in our name. We had created our own obscuring fogs of thought, we had eagerly looked away, we had distracted ourselves from the truth of our exploitation of the world. We knew on some level the imbalance of the world. We knew on some level we were reaching many points of ecological disaster, but we did not listen. We were materially wealthy to the ever-expanding desires and abilities of our human world, and we were spiritually impoverished without limit, but this is all over now. We did not believe that. We refused to believe that to the aliens all humans were humans, primitive in thought, in society, in technology, and from this perspective our wealth, our power, had as little meaning as colour of our skin or size of our nose or shape of our eyes. We had progressed from judging such arbitrary physical qualities, we had known that a black man in Africa is different from a black man in America, we had judged this difference, but we associated without much thought such appearance with an entire culture we could not absorb nor make familiar, and so we remained essentially racist as ever. We thought that the aliens would note our varied appearances and come quickly to the same prejudice. We thought we were the humans the aliens would deal with because we had such familiarity with what we thought advanced technology, though compared to their technology not readily distinguished from magic, our illuminating candle in the dark of ignorance was flickering and overwhelmed by arc lamps of brilliance from the aliens that allowed no shadows. We may have even thought that in time we humans would come to understand and wield this magic. We thought we would learn and even in our human way contribute. We were told by our own human experts that indeed their technology and science were understandable if not replicable by humans at our current level of expertise. We were encouraged. We were hopeful. We thought we had a role. We thought our complex societies had useful organization that they would use to introduce this new world to all those people who were not online, people who had no personal technology, people who were out of the loop and had never had any true representation or voice in our human world. We were wrong. We decided those other humans could remain ignorant and helpless but we would know, we would gather information that is power, we would know and we would act. We had hurriedly convened conferences of experts on cultural interaction, but such was usually corporate or governmental and often corrupt, and such were before dealings with our primitive humans. We have in many cases been inheritors in fact if not in words, of the imperialists, the colonizers, the globalizing forces. We are not judged by the aliens. We are now equally the primitives. We discovered this when our conferences and communications were cast open deliberately, despite rigid security, to anyone who chose to follow our now default, open Internet. We saw our governments fall, we saw stock markets evaporate, we saw money dissolve into numbers, we saw loss of control over flows of information reveal our futility and deceptions and too many secrets previously hidden for the good of our peoples. We saw exponential growth of all those activists who claimed information wanted to be free. We saw information spawning misinformation spawning conspiracy theory spawning conspiracy theories we could apply to this security rupture. We had seen the movies. We tried perhaps to operate as once the human world had ever been, some time ago, some time before, in some places hundreds of years past and in some places as just last week. We found our most secure databases penetrated and infested by worms that had no antidote and no apparent direction or purpose. We thought we could just turn off our electronic reality, but if ever that had been viable strategy in a few days it was impossible. We watched our vast inexistent fields of data not eliminated but flooded, copied and amplified until there was simply too much information. We had access to too much information and too little wisdom. We hoped this was just bugs of our systems adjusting to the alien systems, and in a few days our familiar world would return. We were wrong.

REAL

She is a woman who is calm. She is a woman of many facets but of all she is calm. She is a woman who is daughter, is sister, is wife, is mother, is colleague, is aunt, is grandmother. She is calm from childhood amongst her three sisters, each of whom are different but the same, each of whom are brown skin and black hair of their Hawai'ian heritage, each of whom look like their father and like their mother and like most other people they know as they grow up. She is the second daughter before the third daughter, and the fourth attempt for a son brings yet another daughter, she is not the baby who must be gentled, she is not the eldest whose responsibilities are those of her mother when her mother is not around. She is calm, she is kind, she is brought up this way, she is aware of her mother caring for those impoverished plantation families who are often even more native Hawai'ian, she is aware that this is the way to be, she is aware. She is proud of her father whom she will call Daddy all his life, proud he is loyal, proud he is tall, he is handsome, he is charis-matic, he is lean, he is athletic. She is proud Daddy is able to make friends with almost anyone, is able to lead his own younger brothers, is able to support the family as first a civil engineer and surveyor and then architect. She is proud when she is a child how she and another sister would grasp his biceps and he would laugh and smile, he would raise them up to his shoulders, he would raise them and hold them and call them his girls. She is part of an extended family, most of whom live on the far coast, the windward coast, the wet coast of the island, and as a family they would travel there to visit, but no one else lived on a beach but inland, though this beach is not pleasant to swim as it is down current from the river mouth with brown sand and brown water, down current on this broad bay, here interrupted by an old pier where cane and pineapple were loaded, further along interrupted by what they call the small boat harbour. She is a part of this extended family and briefly the mother of her father would try, as is traditional in Hawai'i, to collect the eldest daughter for companionship, for help, for caring, for transmitting cultural knowledge only grandmothers would know. She knows her mother and Daddy argued over this once, for at this time to be Hawai'ian is not any kind of proudness, at this time she and her sisters are brought up to be Christians, at this time, at home or whenever her mother is around, they must speak proper — that is mainland American — English. She must not speak what her mother the teacher would call pidgin English. She must speak that even, that monotone, that reserved voice of the mainland. She learns both dialects because with her playmates, with her sisters, she will speak local creole that others denigrate as pidgin, local creole that incorporates words of several languages, flowing accents and meanings of several languages, nouns specific, nouns expressive, that is a common dialect that she will switch to easily, even much later as an adult, even on the phone from mainland cities, years later, decades later. She knows her mother only wants them to be accepted and respected by those mainland Americans who perhaps once were ashamed of their own colonial tongue, who perhaps have forgotten how any dialect is living and local and changing. She knows this is only one way her mother protects them. She knows her mother will not allow the eldest daughter to be captured and indoctrinated and lose her Christian propriety by being brought up by the mother of her husband. She knows in this way the unwritten culture of the ancestors is lost bit by bit, for it is not just her mother who is eager to dismiss the older ways, this is a general attitude, a general prejudice, a general prohibition to remember or re-enact the ways of heathen ancestors. She knows Hawai'i is the last island grouping of the Pacific which the Europeans felt they had Discovered, though other island groups of the South Pacific had settled and even for a time traded with these distant cousins, as familiarity in language, as commonality of social structures, of gods, of spirits, proves to the disbelieving first Europeans. She knows that learning this knowledge, learning this past, will engender pride with all those Hawai'ians of Polynesian descent, will engender anew fascination and respect for locals, but this is not the world she knows as a child. She knows only the way the story is told by Europeans and Americans. She knows European contact began here on this beach almost two hundred years past, she knows and will encourage her children to learn this history, she knows something was lost, she knows something else was gained, she knows that her ancestors are mostly indigenous Hawai'ian and some Chinese and the surname is Scot, she knows this is here similar to many other children. She knows the native population of the islands at the time of contact was perhaps four hundred thousand and a hundred years later perhaps forty thousand, as imported disease swept the population, as foreign politics was imposed, and for a time it was thought these natives, these primitives, these godless, these savages, would soon all die out as modern humans from Europe and America came to take over the islands. She knows this is not exactly what happened, she knows then and since local populations married Europeans and Americans and Chinese and Japanese, local populations became, much as her own family, product of many peoples. She knows that there is great distrust of those missionaries who came to the islands, who came to do good, who ended up converting local royalty, who ended up managing vast agricultural lands, who ended up doing very well for themselves. She knows these truths but she does not know these truths. She knows her island of seven major islands of the chain is in the near geographic centre of the northern Pacific, she knows it is the middle of emptiness, knows first that the world is elsewhere, knows soon that the world is all here when the Pacific War begins. She knows there is real fear, real worry, real tension, recalls when she is only a child how there are barbed-wire rolls on the beaches in fear of invasion, she recalls this only as a child, but she does not imagine it actually happening because she feels so safe here with her sisters and her mother and Daddy. She remembers this world as the world of childhood is ever remembered by anyone, as something beyond her to tell anyone but always something to share, something her sisters know, her cousins know, her friends in their small town know. She remembers when the breeze comes from the mountains and when the breeze comes from the ocean. She remembers when the sound of surf is high tide and when it is low tide, a sound so familiar no one notices it but everyone sleeps with that constant sound, in stormy crash or calm whisper. She remembers when all those guava trees drop ripe fruit in the road where it will rot pungent and melt shapeless. She will not like guava because of this memory. She will work in a pineapple factory one summer and learn how to strip horny skin, how to core, how to cut, but even so the fruit is ripe but not rotting, even so she will always enjoy pineapples. She is a woman who was a child who remembers freedom to access beaches around the island, to hike through the fields of pineapples or sugar cane, to hike with no need of guidance, no need of permission, to hike with her sisters and cousins and friends, to open clear beaches. She is a woman who will be sad when later generations will not have this freedom, when bays will be crowded with gigantic houses, when access is begrudgingly allowed down small paths from small roads. She is a woman who is a girl who had never realized just how fortunate a child she had been. She remembers the family spread out across the island, and how this meant constant companionship, constant opportunities for friendship, constant web of kinship, and however stifling or limited she felt, this is nothing more than life in any small town. She is a woman who was a girl, the daughter of a local teacher, but when she is old enough this is not the school she will attend, she will go to the island of Oahu, the island where is Honolulu, where is Pearl Harbor, where is a boarding school for Hawai'ians and part Hawai'ians. She is attending this school, known as King Kamehameha School, as her sisters each attend their respective years. She remembers friends from their small town on summer vacations and fellow students from her island, Kauai, and the other islands, from Maui, from Oahu, from Moloka'i, from Lanai, from the island of Hawai'i, at this boarding school supported by a Trust from ancient Hawai'ian royalty lands as they have been administered by New England missionaries for over a hundred years. She is a woman for whom to grow up and be a young girl in the islands is not exotic or fantastic, however so this will be when she goes to the Mainland for college, however fascinating, however different from the friends she makes and the boys she dates, however yet rare and desired for many people to visit her home islands. She is a woman who is familiar with cultures of mixed descent, she knows the local cuisine of the islands as has remixed influences from everywhere people came to the islands, knows that common starch poi, which is a paste you make from pounding taro — a sort of potato — then dipping to eat with a few fingers or set aside to ferment for a few days then dipping to eat with a few fingers, this common, this simple, this native dish, this nostalgic memory all locals know from childhood on. She knows that people are more than the food they eat, but never that people should not be equal people, that there should ever be the racism of the mainland, however prejudiced could be locals against those called foreigners, those being mostly Caucasian Americans. She is a woman who is the same and different, same as her sisters and her mother and her father and most people she grows up with, indigenous brown skin and black hair of their Hawai'ian heritage, she is a woman for whom racism is a horrific mistake, for whom what racism she might face in California is something to ignore. She is a woman who is calm, who is intelligent but not intellectual, who is open but not fanatic, who is able to remember this young Caucasian man she meets at a college party, who can accept his invitation, who can only look back and marvel that this one night, when she is only twenty and he twenty-five, this night she meets the man she would love and marry and they are equally distant from each their homes. She is wearing a white dress with blue stripes and blue buttons. She does not recall what he is wearing. She is conferring with a few other students about the morality of imposing capital punishment in a current case. She is firm in her argument, she is definite, she is unwavering against assertions that this man, whoever this man is, this man who is raping and murdering, this man when caught deserves to die. She is a woman who insists murder is always wrong, she is a woman who does not believe the threat of death will in any way deter this murderer, that murderer, any murderer, and very certain no one should take upon themselves the right to pronounce death on another. She does not quote scripture but argues from her interpretation of Christianity. She does not feel intimidated by the vehement pronouncement of those who would impose such an irreversible punishment. She does not agree that even confession of such a criminal should summon death, she does not agree he or anyone should summon death, she does not agree that confession is ever enough, for those murderers might be tortured to admit guilt, no she does not agree with any scale of horrors or tortures or multitudes or crimes that the answer is ever death. She insists what everyone here seems to have forgotten as the first prohibition. She makes such an impression on this young master's student from Caltech, this man who knows the joy of finding things out, this student friend of a student friend of a student friend, this stranger, that he will act completely out of character, that he will find out her phone number from the student friend of the student friend who hosted this party, that he will know this simple joy of finding things out by finding out her phone number. She is surprised by his call, she is flattered by his solemnity, she does not at first know who this is, but when he mentions the party and the argument she remembers him. She is a woman who is not familiar with inspiring passion in rather complete strangers, the sort of passion perhaps her more beautiful elder and one younger sister do, but she does agree to see him again. She will scoff at his assertions later, years later, decades later, that he could not imagine why a beautiful girl would be attracted to a boy like him, not a handsome boy, not a rich boy, not anyone like a boy she could have met. She will not like him to denigrate himself even in mild politeness, in typical extensive and proud claims of modesty, typical from his family and childhood, his typical modesty concealing conceit, as if he needs assurance of emotional things he does not know how to find things out. She will date him regularly enough to hear his plans, his goals, his confidence, and learn his droll and dismissive comic tone, though in the beginning of these times, these times to him so unfamiliar, for he has never before dated a girl so seriously, these times in the beginning he is nervous and alternates between proud confidence in his skills, his pursuit of knowledge, and tense certainty he is not good enough for her. She takes him to an orange juice café after the movie, where the drinks are mixed oranges, ice, eggs, and this is to him an entirely new discovery, this cold drink, though later, years later, decades later, he will decide this recipe is no more absurd than hot eggnog. She will bring him many discoveries, she will welcome his embrace, his compliments, his idealization of all romance, but though it is the book of a Scottish lass and her clan in Highland conflicts which perhaps was his first romantic portrayal of women, it is books of Russian classics he gives her, books that give more his view of the world of fathers and sons. She does manage to read some of one of these books, for it seems important to him, though she is not engaged or excited or anything as he might have hoped, but eventually he realizes that what she feels for him needs no literary companions. She will date him regularly and hear of the silver fox farm, of his father, of his elder and younger sisters, of his mother, even as of the last person he struggles angrily with emotions that threaten to bring him to tears, emotions he does not yet want to share, emotions that he will share for she is a kindly listener, she is a woman who is calm, she is so different in this way from of his elder sister or younger sister or his mother. She is a woman who is calm. She teaches him to be polite, as one date when he tells her what this other couple is saying but out of earshot, so demonstrates his skills at reading their lips and faces, until she rebukes him, a mild scolding from which he is ashamed and afraid and her words carry weight she cannot imagine, her words have force and immediacy such he will never read lips again. She cannot imagine how much he wants to please her, as if she were already the woman he will love, he will try to make happy, for the rest of her days. She is impressed that he is a theoretician of physics, she is impressed that he knows the joy of finding things out. She is impressed by his confidence in this abstract realm, this realm that has such a powerful cultural presence but on a popular level known at this time only as source of those atomic bombs that ended the Pacific

War, a popular level of the Cold War, a popular level which then as even later, years later, decades later, is all of which she knows. She listens to his rapt attempts to explain this realm and listens politely but she does not care. She knows it is enough that he cares. She is charmed by his confidence in this realm, by his certainty of moving from master's to doctorate, by his certainty of a career awaiting his completion of education, a career that is modern, is endless, is necessary, a career that will make everything he wants and she wants possible. She knows he is attracted to how exotic she is, the brown skin and black hair of her Hawai'ian ancestry, but it is the invisible but strong presence of her emotional stability, so different from his elder sister and his younger sister and his late mother, this stability greatly attracts him. She is a woman who is calm. She is calm not on occasion or stimulus but always, and this is so new to him, not at all an emotional turbulence, an emotional landscape of hills to climb or cliffs to fall. She is a woman who is calm. She finds this stability is not difficult, though she does not become as eagerly impassioned by the ideas of physics with which he wrests. It is the real world, the married world, her world, she can see as now possible. She recalls the enthusiasm of Daddy, the dreams, the plans, the crushing limits of reality with which her mother would be forced to temper and eventually end those hopes, but the enthusiasm of this young master's student at Caltech admits no limits. She knows that this is all practical possibility. She knows this young master's student is not her father but much more practical. She knows this then loves him, or loves him then knows this, but whichever order, whichever came first, is not something she thinks about. She is a woman who is calm and part of this is accepting and not worrying and not questioning her valid emotions. She does already date other boys, but this is what they are, just boys, and however close in age he is not a boy but a man. She rejects strategy and manipulation, if not outright bargaining and blackmail, that some young women use to capture husbands, to become Mrs Doctor someone, but this is not the way she accepts the young man who knows the joy of finding things out. She knows she will miss him when he is finished his master's and goes somewhere else to finish his doctorate, and so she is not surprised she does miss him, and is pleasantly encouraged when a long letter arrives from him, one letter then two then three which seem to have been written on consecutive days, in which he talks of how much he misses her. She reads his final contention that she and he have to figure something out. She knows the ache of her heart is true and though she does not on his orders keep these letters, she does accept the train fare to take her to the other University. She knows he could have stayed at Caltech but as a country boy he had never liked the pollution of this city, where in the short few blocks walking from his rooms to the laboratory he worked in, every day his eyes would burn, his eyes would tear up, his eyes would see the brown sky beneath the clouds, and the blue sky only a memory. She knows he does not want to compete for funding or position in the vast tracts of American academia, knows that he worries that he might not be as capable as other students there, knows this is not all here motivated by the joy of finding things out. She knows he sits in an open class by a renowned physicist, a man who worked on the project of the atom bomb, who first verbalizes this formulation, this description, of what has always and does now and will always motivate his work. She knows later, years later, decades later, he will read about this man, and he will say it is always the joy of finding things out. She knows by this accomplished time, as Professor, he will realize he has in fact done more or discovered more or written more than those fellow students he had thought were superior. She knows he knows this only later. She knows only that he wants to leave this place. She knows this city of cars is worse than he could have imagined, where you could drive for hours and never leave urban or suburban lands, and so far from the ocean breeze and clear skies of the islands on which she grew up, so it might have been already a hope that following him meant she would never return here. She knows that in being with him there is the chance she will not need to return, and in fact this is what happens. She reads his love letters. She is a woman who is calm, and knows he is not a man to exaggerate or feign his emotions, for though he is so very smart intellectually she knows there are things he does not know, she knows he loves to find things out but also that there are things he will avoid because of the unpredictable emotions they raise. She knows him enough to trust him when he professes love. She comes to this city and meets two people his mother had taught years earlier as a visiting teacher in one-room schoolhouse years before her marriage, healthy years before his birth, who will help her to adjust to married life and responsibility, who will tell her what clothes she needs for winter, who will teach the favourite dish of her husband, who will serve as family here so far from the families of her youth and his youth. She had never before seen snow. She had never seen the world covered in frozen blankets that soften all corners and look so comfortable but are in fact icy cold. She will adjust to this land, this weather, these brief winter evenings and these long summer evenings. She knows she has made the right choice and does not regret those boys left behind. She knows when he promises to do his best to make her happy she can trust him, she can only promise to do her best to make him happy. She follows him to this University where he garners his doctorate, then this other University to enter his career, this place where he gains tenure, this place where there are so many others who know the joy of finding things out, this place from which she and her husband come to her home island with an infant girl and a baby boy. She is here for Christmas. She is pleased to see her others sisters all married as well. She is proud Daddy and Mama are now even more grandparents with her children added, that Daddy is impressed and likes her husband, that it does not matter everyone does not know that he finds joy in figuring things out, that his profession is admired anyway. She guides him into her extended family and they visit around the island and treat him to traditional food and then gathering feast where the pig, the fish, the laulau are buried in a sand oven on the beach, where it cooks all day, is dug open and shared around, shared with poi, shared with raw fish, shared with typical local family spirit that is honest and real however much the tourist industry uses it later to entrance visitors. She knows this place is where she came from and where she will visit with husband and family each year as the children grow up. She stays home when the children are small but after arranging with a neighbour to feed the children lunches during the school year, she returns to finish her education degree and become like her mother a teacher, then saving enough income that they live well, that they can now afford these yearly visits to the islands. She knows the flight is one cost but that they will always stay with her parents at the house Daddy designed to replace the house in which she had grown up. She has made this possible for him and the children as he has made possible for her and the children. She follows him in his career, from this university on sabbatical to this other university to that university, first seven years, again seven years when he will work at the University in Honolulu and they will live on the island of Oahu, will visit her home island, visit two others on vacations, but it is the small town and the brown beach sand and brown water her children know best. She knows it seems absurd to her nieces and nephews that her children will always change and run out to the beach, whatever the weather, whatever the water, and dive into the brown water and laugh and play. She knows it seems absurd but they have just come from a world-size freezer where water is white and cold and layers over everything, with weather none of these relatives could yet imagine, where to come to the islands is a promise and a dream, where the first thing to know is if you went swimming. She knows that it is a yearly visit but soon these years fly past so quickly, she knows only the promise of the future for her children, she knows that this is what family is for, she knows this is the nature of time, she knows it is a process of loss even so much as she has gained. She knows as years go by between each return there will be fewer of the extended family she had known, but there will be children she does not yet know. She is a calm woman. She knows this is the way life progresses, not time as a set quantity running down, running out, in your personal hourglass, but time running up, becoming different not in quantity but quality, until it is a full life, and who will claim to know when that is for anyone. She knows this but she does not know this. She does not argue this insight with anyone. She does not know time as simply one variable on any graph or vector or however scientists might measure it. She knows time as something that cannot be so reduced to increments of something that is always the same, for this is not what her life is, what life is for her husband, should he choose to think of its emotional qualities, for moments of pleasure can seem so fleeting and moments of anguish so distended and moments of boredom long and moments of interest brief. She knows this in life is like reading a book where days months years may pass unnoticed, where crucial afternoons might persist for such time that their moments are greater than any of those days months years. She knows this the year she must stay home with the youngest alone, when he is fascinated by the cooking shows she watches, when he is curious of the soap opera she watches, and it is then she determines to return to university and finish her degree and master's in Education. She will not become a housewife who watches soap operas and is involved in sordid suburban boredom and emotional games, and it is only as her own parents had sent her and her sisters off to school, that she feels it is equally appropriate to send her own children to the neighbourhood school. She also notices there is always a chronological gap in the woven texture of soap operas, a chronological emptiness of the time children are young, the time actual marriages mature, the time children grow up, and none of this is the world. She knows the world is not a soap opera. She knows this later, years later, decades later, when she watches the girl graduate and the boy graduate, and it does not seem possible so many years have passed. She knows this but she does not know this. She survives the death of her mother and years later of Daddy, and she is deeply sad, sorrowful in a way she has never imagined, in a way she can only hold on to her husband and beg him not to leave, in a way she realizes this must be, she must be, for there is no other way to mourn but mourn and this is the way it must be. She is a calm woman. She does not pressure her children for accomplishment as her husband does not, remembering his own competitive youth, constant questioning why he was not doing as well as his elder sister in English, constant questioning why his younger sister was not doing as well as he in Math, and he does not want his own children wracked by such academic anxieties. She is more concerned with their kindness and their compassion and how well they get along with their peers. She has expectations. She does not pressure but she and her husband are unable to not harbour expectations. She is intelligent if not intellectual and her husband is both. She knows there must be expectations but it is the younger, the boy, who will flaunt his weak math and implicitly claim his artistic temperament, this artistic temperament that does not fail to be intellectual, that all the same might not be artistic, that resembles Daddy in act as much as appearance. She knows he would like to be like Daddy. She knows he is not. She knows how he and his elder sister are different from each other, different but the same, different as unique combinations of her and a man who enjoys finding things out. She knows both his artistic elder sister and artistic younger sister sometimes worry that the boy is growing up in an oppressively scientific household, but there is nothing to do, there is only her certainty that this concern is extreme invention, that truly she and her husband are offering the best upbringing possible. She knows the life they have given him is the best they can, and that he seems to puzzle his father as much as the daughter is so much more understandable, is not in the least artistic or excessively intellectual, does not trouble either of them. She knows that to care without time limit is the nature of being a parent, for a child is always a child, a parent is always a parent. She knows the daughter persists on an accomplished trail to adulthood as first a biology student and soon a doctor. She is proud of her, confident of her, even as the boy continues to wander, continues to puzzle, continues to promise potential but as a seed or nut or acorn cast on the ground, only the future will reveal confidence worthwhile. She knows that not all fields are fertile nor that all seeds prosper but there is a vehement certainty the boy carries, for he will listen to the arguments, he will dismiss them, he will do what he has always wanted. She knows he is able to make friends with anyone, knows he applies social skills easily and intelligently, and she does not see what it is that hinders him from accomplishing those reasonable goals, those goals to become an architect like Daddy, to become a professional of some sort like his father. She knows he has the intelligence but not the confidence for some reason. She knows this but does not know this. She knows she is still his mother. She knows this when he is a young adult, when he no longer lives at home, when he lives with a young woman, when she worries about him that another woman should worry about him. She knows this when they break up. She had hoped they would marry and two years is long enough for common-law, but he goes to another city, he goes to no program, no friends, no school, only another place. She knows this bothers her husband as it worries her but both have confidence he will survive and maybe even prosper away from home, away from his anxious parents, and after all, this might be necessary for an artist. She knows her husband fears they will never see him again, fears he has done something wrong, fears he has failed as a father but such determination is for the future. She knows he has grown up but not grown up. She knows he is now and perhaps will ever be a puzzle. She sends Christmas letters and gifts he must open individually each for twelve days before the day, she does not know what else to do, she does not know what she and her husband could possibly do now, she does not know if ever you are beyond being a parent, she only hopes he will somehow survive well. She knows this does not happen and so a year later his father brings him home. She knows the family is troubled because the boy is troubled and only a boy not yet a man. She knows emotions do not know time and for this reason his past is not past but every day present, and he still seems unable to flourish, unable to become the man the boy ever promised to be. She knows this as her husband knows this but neither they nor anyone else knows how to help the boy, and so a year later he will have the brain injury that puts him in a coma. She knows he will survive the coma for if not she will have failed to be a mother, she knows then she is a mother, she knows, she knows her husband collapses in tears one night it seems the boy will die, she knows she must not fail as a wife, so she returns to her interpretation of Christianity, there is nothing else to do. She is a woman who is calm. She prays.

RESERVE

When they first came to be on the Reserve it did not seem too different from the way they had always lived. They had once lived in suburbs and bedroom communities safe from the awkward civic cauldron of the Cities, and now it was only that there was no City, or rather no connection to the City for that place had continued but become stranger than ever before. They had not exactly fled the city, but had become secure on the Reserve. They had a level of security prosecuted mostly by drones, in more recent years piloted, maintained, armed, by the relevant artificial intelligence, that node of the artificial intelligence which governed what was now the Reserve. They had suffered during the night of the arrival of the aliens, when their most secure and protected electromagnetic network was mysteriously invaded, momentarily crashed, and the usual functions in water, in sewage, in traffic, in firemen, in police, came to stop. They were more fortunate than other humans in that their advanced logical sky was quickly rebooted, and but for the few wandering or stopped vehicle traffic early in the morning, no one was seriously inconvenienced. They watched their streaming of far-seeing news that displayed the furious disruption of other places, even a few in the modern postindustrial world, but again those were Cities. They congratulated themselves for having the foresight, the caution, the wisdom of having backup systems easily started, though these were once designed by the military to allow information flows even under stress of atomic war. They realized this original network had multiplied and mutated to serve many civilian services, even if the most apparent was offering globalized merchants, further ironic proof that capitalism was the best way to organize our complex human culture. They were proud of their measured response to the aliens. They were proud that unlike so many Cities, they felt this was a smooth transition to the advent, they even allowed themselves to believe this was indicative of how smooth their human history would now incorporate the aliens, they even thought that in their obvious dominance of the human world the aliens would come to work through them. They were not wrong but not exactly right. They saw the horror of the advent as a promise that they would survive, the Cities burning, the wars religious and territorial and ideological and economic, but these conflicts were far away and in their gated and defended communities they had little immediate fear. They saw too late the dissolution of their power over flows of information power, they saw governments fall, they saw stock markets evaporate, they saw money dissolve into numbers, they saw futility and deceptions and too many secrets. They passed through cleansing fire, for the physical and information universe was still there, and in a typical human resolution those humans closest to actual power over other humans decided the answer was to continue everything exactly as before. They faced down the chaos and decided that they were immortal and no revolution would unseat them, even provoked by the advent of the aliens. They decided to act as if nothing had changed. They were able to sustain this lie throughout their globalized Internet world, because it was clear there must be an organizing principle with which to answer in voice of all humans. They decided they knew how humans are humans, how an economy of scarcity such as had in their world animated humans for hundreds of years, and sometimes just last week, was the innovation that made them who they were. They saw that the answer was to incorporate the aliens in the only world that truly mattered, the world that made them modern humans, the world in which such a vanishingly small percentage of humans dominated other humans, and of course this world was economic. They decided to trade. They realized that there must be customers and sources, desires and fulfilment, scarcity and debt, but this was only for humans to trade with humans. They realized that any alien with easy technology to transcend light speed could probably manufacture all its needs, so what could they offer, what would the aliens take, where was the market, and what had value to the aliens. They did not ask the farmers for it was only humans the peasants fed. They did not ask the manufacturers because truly the aliens were able to create many things with such facility, such speed and volume, as they demonstrated in offering our engineers how to create to further create, but this did not seem in exchange, as the aliens did not ask for anything in turn. They did not ask the military, as much as military voices would avidly desire powerful new weaponry, for there was nothing to value in trade. They did not ask philosophers, who were apparently entirely happy that thought would be exchanged for no monetary recompense, who were happy that even to the aliens they might share thoughts. They were confused. They were even briefly on the verge of a conceptual breakthrough, discovering the economic world is not the only world that matters. They immediately sensed that the aliens had things humans would desire, even if they could only form them after generations of generations of technology, had created them physically here on earth. They could not be satisfied with the technology of which we were most proud, and they did not know what else could be valued. They came in the end to discover those radically useless humans called 'artists' to have some use after all. They discovered the aliens wanted art. They did not want common reproductions, unless such manifestation was in fact part of the argument for it to be art, they were not satisfied by whatever senses their drones could send while visiting this or that gallery, they were childishly attracted to something called the aura of a work of art. They who traded found this could not be duplicated for trade.

RESET

When the aliens came it was not where we expected. When the aliens came it was all over the earth, as many or some or all came where we were not waiting and we were not ready. We could have welcomed the aliens as all strangers had been welcomed in the first contact with other humans by humans. We thought major cities or icons or even megastructures like dams or walls or towers would be where they came first. We thought there had to be some observable constant or important quality but these meant less than nothing. We thought our world had centres of spiritual value even if only that so many people came to gaze and be in the presence of our highest spiritual memories, Stonehenge, Athenian Parthenon, Pyramids of Giza, the Vatican, Millau Viaduct, Temple of the Mount, Angkor Wat, Sun Temple at Konark, Palaces at Persepolis, Red Fort at Delhi, Taj Mahal, Mount Everest, White Horse Temple, Mount Fuji, Tikal, Machu Picchu, Teotihuacan, Tenochtitlan, Cahokia, all, all, all such places. We had seen the movies. We discovered the aliens were not tourists. We did not understand. We discovered the concept 'where' relied on 'here' and 'there', and as such did not apply to the aliens, not in material presence, not in virtual haunting, not in any recognizable way. We knew only multiple Cartesian coordinates, invisible planes, insensible points, when we were told it was lived orientations that found them, we were told the aliens were in front of us and beside us and behind us. We did not understand. Some people searched for somewhere the aliens had not and we hoped never would reach, but the aliens were already where and whenever. We saw that our world, our borders, our territories, our geography, our barriers, were of no consequence to the aliens. We saw where there was nowhere to hide. We saw this for everyone when the aliens came, and our many plans to create an independent human underground, our certainty there was somewhere to hide and something to do, was revealed as pathetic and human, all too human. We did not as individual humans encounter the aliens but also not as groups, not in a way we could explain, nothing rational, and this was stimulus to imagine with hope that this was all mass hallucination. We seemed to share remarkable consistency at least in their alien attitude, their friendly approach, their concern we humans would know we were not insane. We were later told that continuing to live as though nothing had changed, continuing to act as though nothing had happened, was in fact the definition of insanity. We were told this by the aliens through the mediums of our humans most concerned with the metaphysical reality, and revealed knowledge of religion proved excellent grounding for those humans we called priests or imams or monks or shamans or psychotherapists. We called this encounter with the aliens the 'Advent', as it is named in all our varied dictionary definitions, for the arrival of a notable person or thing, for something means that it is finally here, for coming or arrival of something or someone that is important or worthy of note, for the fact of an event happening, an invention being made, or a person arriving, for an arrival or coming, for the introduction of a new product, idea, custom, for a coming into place, view, or being, even for the period beginning four Sundays before Christmas and observed by some Christians as a season of prayer and fasting, for the first or the expected second coming of Christ, for the coming of Christ at the Incarnation, though ideas did not persist long that the aliens were Christ or Christians or for other hopeful followers that the aliens were Mohammed or that the aliens were Maitreya Buddha of the future or any of our many human gods or God, however we had named them, worshipped them, sacrificed for, killed for, martyred ourselves, begged for their succour, or asked for the destruction of unbelievers or believers in other gods or God or godlessness. We called the advent of the aliens many other terms, we offered prepositional values, we used or did not use capitals for it was impossible there could be another event that we would mean. We found other words even in English, we called it arrival, coming, onset, appearance, approach, entrance, occurrence, visitation, event, contact, and of course there were all the synonyms in all those other languages that confused humans before the aliens came. We thought that this would diminish religious sentiment but in fact the predictable existential fact was that it sparked new religious sentiments, that it resurrected some dying faiths and combined some others. We found religion flourishing everywhere though these aliens seemed to have no concern with our souls, no revelations of ethical worlds or metaphysical structures or meaning to our human lives, and some of our mediums were more practically satisfied with money or power. We knew some people called this advent supernatural, some people called this paranormal, some people insisted that this was here and now that true and final reality. We refused to believe this. We were convinced that as one world once covered a real world, the rhetoric of armed preparation and propaganda insisting on how subhuman were our enemies, godless, infidel, tyrannical, would be later revealed as simply wartime propaganda, would be later revealed as cynical realpolitik, so this so-called final reality would also be eventually dispelled. We had seen the movies. We forgot they were alien so did not have the slightest concern for what was real, only a touching concern for the fragility of all those worlds of music and dancing and all athletic arts, and concern for all those models of the universe, all our ideas of reality of which we must not allow ourselves to think we were now insane. We were in no way insane. We thought this would be better. We were wrong.

REAL

She is the sister who has always done the right thing. She is older but only by two years, she learns to care from her mother, she learns that to care is not expected by her mother and her father. She is mature, she is a girl, she has an aptitude for caring, and all these are qualities that lead her to become a doctor. She is a woman who cares who learns as a girl to care. She leads her little brother in crossing the safety lights on the way to their neigbourhood school. She protects him from the cigarettes and later the alcohol and later yet other recreational drugs. She watches him and watches out for him and this is constant vigilance, for he is a curious and friendly and sensitive boy who always looks to her to lead in play. She is his only and he is her only constant playmate as they move from city to city growing up following the career of her father. She does not have the same scepticism necessary to someone who enjoys figuring things out. She does not question. She learns quickly the rules of the road and follows the directions given, never much deviating to unknown paths, never much looking up from the path at her feet but for seeing it extend to the horizon, which must be a worthwhile goal, because the path leads to it. She is the sister who has always done the right thing. She plays with him, she finds others to play all together, she is comfortable in being the axis around which he orbits, sometime near and quickly, sometime far away leisurely, and she always tries to be there for him when no one else is. She invents romantic medieval clashes using her dolls and his action figures, but the scales are often different, and perhaps the narratives they imagine are essentially different too. She knows her dolls are all part of a family and conflicts borrowed from soap operas occupy their days, but he insists his dolls are not dolls but action figures who live not in families but are constantly flying to other planets and battling aliens and fighting those typical wars, where motivations are obscure or forgotten and the purpose of pillows, beds, chairs, tables, any furniture is to create fortresses or spaceships. She watches as he does the same science fantasy popular culture, but she does not change it, make it hers personally, and maybe it is something only boys do in cataloguing wonders and arguing statistics. She is comfortable in the world given, the fantasy aspects, and begins to read those better literary works that centre around romances, even though this is not something he follows, and she is gone like the wind, she is widow of a Frenchman, she is always in her mind playing a favourite game. She is becoming a teenager while he is taking apart those imagined worlds, but he does not know it is emotion desired by readers, not faster spaceships, not swords of light, not worlds too different from her own. She plays with him anyway and keeps her dolls' unspoken various motivations, allegiances, hatreds, emotions of any sort. Soon she will form close friendships with older children, older boys. She learns these others are not as pliable and obedient as her younger brother, and in this she enjoys ceding control or imagination or direction of whatever play will be. She does not forget her younger little brother, but they are as different as her calm mother warns, though for their childhood younger little brother and elder sister remain close and shy with relatives and sensitive and intelligent. She changes when the change comes in ways her little brother does not understand. She begins to become like the confusing girls he knows at school and not his elder sister. She is reading and living in worlds inaccessible but not very interesting to him, in history and pageantry, in royalty and wars of succession, in gallant knights of whatever realm and their chaste princesses awaiting their heralded return. She knows her little brother finds these stories and these worlds boring if not offensive, for he never comes along there, he never thrills to discover simple human motivations of love and longing and hatred and villainy. She suspects he in fact remains the sensitive and emotional child her younger little brother has ever been, but this is pushed aside with great force, this is denied in any group, this is not the face he wishes to present to the world. She knows herself a far simpler person in this way. She always presents herself as herself and never has devised a character such as they use in playing roles, she always runs the game, designs the castles or caverns, she violates her own rules in order that her little brother and their friends can persist in the dungeons against the dragons. She reads and creates according to the usual genre 'fantasy' of descent through whatever mutations, from the worlds created by that Oxford philologist before she can even understand what is that discipline, but when she learns she does not decide to read the varied mythic sources but to read parallel works, works which dominate that genre, worlds of simplified middle ages politics, worlds of kings and queens and princes and princesses, worlds of such technology of tempered swords and longbows and maces and crossbows, worlds of recognizable social structures of nobles and peasants and priesthood, worlds where the rules of conduct are clear and distinct even as the geography is invented and conflicts and politics never as complex but equivalent to local technology. She reads some history books, she tries to make it plausible, but there is no way to rationalize dragons and elves and hobbits and orcs and magic and after a while she does not care. She is following the rules. She reads these books and uses certain imaginary sites, certain castles, certain cities, certain invented geography, to give her little brother worlds to inhabit and play in even as it becomes clear he would rather create his own worlds. She watches him draw scenes of such inspiration even as he looks at pictures in fantasy worlds, worlds that include unicorns and Pegasus and magic in all forms, but he is never pleased with any representational felicity even as she tells him that they are so good, that as there are no models or reality but only conceptual images, images borrowed from this book or that book, this calendar or that calendar, it can hardly be said they do not look the way they really look. She has an idea she wants him to complete but after a time he wants to create his own stories, using the game characters, the game world, and then soon he wants to create his own characters, his own game worlds. She knows this is the way to spend an open Sunday afternoon. She knows he knows this as well until his creative impulses seem to get the better of his control and he is thinking as he draws, as he draws spaceships and aliens and robots. She does not know why he no more draws horses or knights or magicians, drawing only over and over a blonde, graceful, beautiful elf maiden — but he does not share this image, he does not have a story for her, he does not bring someone to rescue her from this dark unformed evil which could be a monster or could be human. She does not ever understand his artistic urges and in time this will not matter. She knows this is when she begins to lose her little brother but also when she knows she will never lose her little brother. She is the sister who has always done the right thing. She wants him and he wants her to like each their friends but this is not the case. She has boyfriends he does not like. She is as beautiful as their mother but different in her fortunes with boys becoming men. She is also as calm and also knows the joy of finding things out, but never applies her thought to what she deserves, what she should receive, what she is worth, from all the boys not yet men. She goes on a trip to China when she is only fifteen and when she returns she is different in subtle or persistent ways, ways neither her mother so calm, her father finding out about other physics, her little brother can understand. She returns smoking. She returns attached to older boys though this is not unusual. She returns ever more committed to appear adult and this does not include the same games with her little brother, though she does persist, she does enjoy, she does create and control further role-playing games, but this is now with other boys, older boys, and whatever games or plans she shared with her little brother are now forgotten. She has friends he does not like. She is out late but she has different friends and different interests and though this has always been the possibility, this is as they become youths the more usual case. She wonders how lonely he must be as he wonders how she is serving others and not herself. She rests outside school to talk about soaps and all the trivial and contradictory storylines and characters, to invent or understand her own life and that of her girlfriends alone as somehow so defined, though there is one boy, a smart boy, a friendly boy, a boy they first wonder if he is gay, who will incisively note how their lives are not a soap opera, not that soap opera set in a hospital or unstated businesses, not those later evening shows which are all soap operas but in name, not any soap opera, but she and her girlfriends dismiss his analysis. She does agree somewhat but also feels the boy is just a boy, for imagination is at play and not documentary realism. She will study this in a course at the University, the one course in Social Sciences that is required for pre-med, but at this time her loyalty to the entire world of daytime soaps is not connected to the various psychological or political or artistic lenses that course offers. She enjoys finding things out, in this case and that case, on this program and on that program, sharing as is necessary with her friends some invented sense of emotions. She wants to explain this to her little brother, who seems to harbour the same mistaken apprehension, the same meaningless dismissal, the same perceptual deficit in expecting popular culture to enrich rather than distract from this world. She could argue the same of all the boys playing football or basketball or hockey, could argue however they claim this reveals the truth of winners and losers, the truth of the world, this is an impoverished conception of the world. She could argue there is truth in ambiguity. She could argue that all these soap opera characters with fluctuating emotional directions and loyalties actually are more true, more real, more rewarding as a picture of this adult world, than those limited games rigidly held within arbitrary lines and arbitrary times, which always seems to involve simple or complicated, individual or group control and movement of some kind of ball. She does not appreciate sports even in the minimal way as do her father or her little brother. She thinks sports are absurd. She believes that the interesting aspects of teams in any sport are in fact the complex dynamics within and between teams, are in fact more soap opera, in fact how spectators claim this allegiance or that allegiance, in fact how such sports serve as no more than ritualized birth of hierarchy, in fact serve to identify this boy against all other boys. She is not attracted to boys who play sports but goes along silently in order to sustain emotional and social friendships with all those girls who do find them attractive. She could argue this with her little brother but in fact never does. She could argue with her mother or father but never does. She is the sister who always does the right thing. She works and studies and worries about her weight. She wants to learn the rules and follow the rules and succeed through the rules. She is the sister who has always done the right thing. She feels strong concerns for her little brother for it seems he is losing what usual social contacts as are necessary. She worries that he is wandering in thought and behaviour and if no one else is concerned, she will be. She watches and listens and worries as she becomes a young woman. She wonders what it is he draws or paints or thinks about, but by this age their individual tastes, their individual tendencies, have become as separate, as private, as shielded and unknown to the other, for there is always the girl he loves but she does not appear to be any of the girls he knows. She knows some girls like him, but he seems oblivious, seems clumsy, seems removed, and in all these aspects of his personality, all these ways, he does not get to know the true emotional terrain of an adult. She loves her little brother and wants to help him. She is aware that it is not with girls she can help him. She is aware he does not like her friends as he is convinced none are worthy of his friendship. She watches him through high school but there seems little she can do. She finds him a job at a grocery store where she works and he is there for a month or two but then basketball season arrives and he needs time to go to practice and time to go to games. She finds him a job as a waiter but he does not stay even a week past training. She sees him survive high school and enter university only two years after her, but from the beginning his selfishness drives him into perhaps the least immediately and perhaps the least eventually practical disciplines, if discipline is what you could call art, if discipline can be so nearly identical to wasting time. She has to admit she does not understand him, even when he takes classes in something called communications. She has to recognize how different they are. She wants a car so saves her money from the supermarket and buys a used compact. She sees her little brother needs a car when he moves out to live with a girlfriend and his father gives him one of their family cars. She is not sure about this girlfriend though her mother calmly decides her son will marry her. She knows the girl is attractive physically and at least intelligent enough to be a university student, but she senses how her little brother and she are posing a perfect relationship and does not know if this goes beyond how she looks. She believes her little brother is intelligent and social but he seems unconcerned that others might view him as manipulative. She is not too surprised that in two years they break up. She is not too surprised he does not flourish well simply by being in another city. She is by this time finishing school as a doctor and has found a man she loves and marries and soon brings their first child into the world. She is eager to return to work after two months three months four months, and her mother is calm when she learns that for promoting the career of her husband they must move across the country. She wishes on some days her father would admit even the slightest professional pride. She suspects once again this is her father being rigorously balanced in approval of his daughter and his son. She has always been a very good student, she has always been a very kind student, she has always looked out for her little brother, she has progressed through pre-med and then medical school on a scholarship, she has found the right man and borne children to make her parents grand. She does not complain, does not allow uncertainty, does not act in any superior manner. She loves her little brother, no matter what he does, no matter what he does not, which seems to be not a lot. She is the sister who has always done the right thing. She does not know if this is true of her little brother, who seems to do little of anything, who seems to use his intelligence and charm in attracting young women and promising little but how more he will use them. She knows he says he will be an artist but of what kind even he does not know, and he has never used family connections, never used his aunts, never asked for any-thing like reasonable advice. She does not understand. She knows he is troubled and this is enough, this seems necessary if not sufficient to be an artist, this seems to have been so from their childhood, though she cannot recall any traumatic event that should hinder his maturity, hinder his expression, hinder his skills. She does not feel she can help, if even she knew what that help would be, and by now they are grown up and they have their separate lives, by now what little difference in temperament, difference in attitude, difference in desires, is nearly impassable. She loves her little brother but she also loves her parents and her husband and her children. She has her own concerns. She will be in the city of her in-laws and soon the child will know her grandmother is mother of her husband and not of her mother. She is only briefly concerned for this is the way the world turns and there are never any guarantees. She is surprised at the first by how demonstrative and emotional his family is, how different from the calm she grew up in, how different he is now, how different the world is now. She is a doctor of general practice but is not interested in specializing or determining any social gains from her position, though she does attend some conferences when she represents the hospital in which she works, though she finds the same bonhomie and childish conflicts she had known when studying, though she hears more than ever from the American doctors about how much money they make, or the size of their houses, the make of their cars, the places they go on vacation. She wonders if she is naïve, for her pleasure in being a doctor is pleasure in being a doctor. She is a woman who enjoys finding things out as much as her father. She enjoys finding things out in a more practical sphere of injuries and healing and rehabilitation. She knows she is regarded well by her colleagues and usually seen by her patients as friendly rather than intimidating. She is proud of this. She is never much tempted by offers of money and power and better golf courses by recruiting firms from down south, though it is flattering. She would not want to go anywhere that would deflect the onward career of her husband. She is also proud of this. She is the sister who has always done the right thing. She does not know if this is true of her little brother. She is always sceptical of the women he finds. She almost wants to be an elder sister to the woman and warn her off, warn her not to have reasonable expectations of her little brother, not to look for marriage, look for children, look for progress in the yet unknown career. She almost wants to be this way but then she realizes how much she loves her little brother. She is the sister who has always done the right thing. She loves her little brother. She realizes this once again when the phone rings early one morning and her mother tells her that her little brother has suffered a brain injury and is at the moment in a coma. She listens to her mother but in talking emotions seem to well up and her mother can no longer speak but only weep. She knows her mother is crying the way she had when her mother and Daddy died, but this is more sudden, more unexpected, more devastating. She waits. She listens to her father and the fragile sphere of emotions is left implicit, now when it is more necessary to know the hospital, the doctor, the injury, the unspoken plea that she come home. She goes home alone. She sees her mother weep at the slightest thought of her little brother, then seem to summon her emotions deliberately by looking at pictures, pictures from this city and that city, pictures of Honolulu, pictures of all the times they went to the islands. She hears that her father cried. She hears from her father with something like awe that it was uncontrollable, unexpected, unlike anything he had ever known before. She is not alone unable to imagine her father so moved. She listens to family friends who say her father has become much more open now, much more emotional, much more gentle and kindly, much more that he will now listen to other people. She is a woman who knows the joy of finding things out and he is a man who knows the joy of finding things out. She is a doctor so her enquiries are educated and she can hear the doubts and sense the caution in the replies. She discovers one of the doctors here was a student of her father several years before and he wants to be helpful, but in truth as always with a brain injury there is persistent ignorance, for every brain injury is the same and every brain injury is different. She knows there is not much to know and no joy in what they do know. She knows they do not even know at first if he will survive, and they do not know how he will survive. She recognizes the apparent correlation between the extent of brain damage and the length of the coma. She waits with some anxiety. She wants to be more certain, she wants to bear good news, but she knows some answers will only be known after her little brother comes out of the coma. She knows that no one knows how to bring him out of this persistent sleep that is not sleep. She waits here with her parents for one week but her life must continue, so she will leave for the other side of the country where her husband waits and her daughter waits. She accepts this is the way things will go. She thinks of leading her little brother in games, in crossing the big road on the way to school, in playing as mistress of dungeons and rancher of dragons, in helping him to this job then this later job, in watching with surprise and only a little disapproval when his smile catches unwary girls. She thinks of him with great love. She walks down the quiet hallways of the neuro-critical care ward, walks slowly, walks thoughtfully, walks as if time will then slow down, walks in childhood bargaining that her little brother will wake up if she walks only on these dark tiles. She finds her mother in the quiet room. She sits beside her mother. She sees that her mother is struggling to remain calm and wonders how this could ever be a struggle, for her mother is a woman who is calm, who is always calm, who has forever been calm. She decides she will believe in God if their prayers are answered. She will now have her own children and watches them grow up perhaps with fewer expectations than she or her little brother had. She will know her husband is not so equivocal, will know he encourages the daughters and the son, will know he makes no secret of forgiving her everything and, in the interest of forging masculinity, for-giving nothing of his son. She will have her daughter become a paramedic, a first responder, and this daughter will have no thwarted ambitions to become a doctor, this daughter will be comfortable working on that most immediately practical, that most urgent, that most rewarding aspect of medicine, where the rules and goals, the success and failure, of her work is something that arises more than once a day. She enjoys finding things out by rescuing the injured. She is as calm as her grandmother in accepting survival and loss and the sharp definition of the two, though after delivering the patient to the hospital she, no more than the nurses in critical care, no more than the therapists in critical rehabilitation, will know the ultimate outcome in which she has served as an integral part. She knows that her job per-forms the same actions, though many years later, as the night her uncle went into the coma. She knows but does not know, for no one speaks of this but often alludes to this past event as nothing less than a miracle. She knows her uncle will refuse this characterization and insist that all was a matter of luck and a matter of potentials met by those people who worked on him, by those machines designed for aid, by even the trained aid of summoned paramedics who are not much different than her. She tells him this luck was so consistent it might be best known as a miracle, but to this he offers no more than a shrug. She will marry and have children by a fireman and this is no less than the life one leads, the life one expects, the life one appreciates before the advent and the aliens. She knows her sister and her brother and most people she knows will not likely suffer such injury and coma as he had, not know if this helps, this hinders, this means anything, after the advent. She is also the other daughter who becomes a wildlife officer, who is to marry another woman, a situation that surprises no one, for she has always been a tomboy and never a little princess, but she does not know if this helps, this hinders, this means anything, after the advent. She is the sister of a brother who becomes a contractor, a man who works with tools, a man who has no trouble distinguishing what is a tool and what is a human, though such is never a question that arises for him. She will see one of her daughters marry and bring forth a child, she will see her son's wife add to the grandchildren, she will see the other daughter's wife also bring forth a child through human technology before even the advent comes. She will have her career, her respect, her responsibility, and will not determine how they will be a family. She will not interfere and though over the years the children do visit the islands and meet their cousins in the extended family, this will be nowhere near as often as she and her little brother had once gone, so to the extent they will be part Hawai'ian this will become a unique explanation for their cheekbones, their colouring, the history of their mother. She will allow herself some pride in how well they will be at school. She will forgo this pleasant imagined future as a last temptation for a normal life, a very lucky, very generous, very desired life. She will forgo this imagined future if her little brother will just wake up now. She joins her mother in a prayer.

RESERVE

When they first came to be on the Reserve it did not seem too different from the way they had always thought. They had always been most comfortable socially around people like themselves, at least in the early stages of adult life, after some adventures in the Cities during their youth, and before that they had lived wherever their guardian lived. They told themselves that they were not racist or even conservative but only like everyone else, and they were not bad people around here, just had never had the opportunity to be conspicuously good. They were separate and equal. They had lived on the Reserve when it was called a suburb or a town or something like that, Views or Heights or Woods or Valley or Lakes, whatever minor geographical anomaly that could be the identifying feature and offer some manufactured status or history. They were here before the aliens came and when the aliens came and they hoped to be here after the aliens left. They might have some curiosity about the aliens, but there were endless sources for information about them, there were videos, documentaries, articles in magazines, on websites, even a selection of books. They did not often go to the library, but considered themselves moderately informed. They were sincere but not falsely effusive when they proclaimed that they were all human now, whether their skin was darker, or nose larger, or eyes rounder, yes, they had no time for systemic racism that seemed to plague the Cities even after the aliens arrived. They would argue their generous attitude with those few others that the suburb might once have discriminated against, who were now so openly courted, because they were all human after all. They would sometimes even argue that they would be glad to have one of the aliens pick their Reserve as home, though nobody knows how they choose, how they decide, what they would want in living besides humans. They would often display and offer 'shots' of the alien substance so popular amongst the younger crowd, the kind which was officially prohibited on the Reserve, the kind that in some way operated exactly as the user's deepest desires wanted, as narcotic, as hallucinogen, as psychoactive of any sort. They would say this substance was new or more original or anything that titillated fellow part-goers, but no one could say for sure what it was until it was too late, and some humans were so afraid of what it might reveal of them that they refused a shot or claimed allergy or being already drugged. They would worry, but in fact the shot was never poisonous or even momentarily dangerous to humans. They might recognize their social life on the Reserve emulated that golden era of the nineteen fifties, that this might have been on purpose, that increasing material wealth was always filling any sort of spiritual emptiness. They were not concerned with the world away, the whole world of the Cities, and indeed those who had something like a career never had to pass the gates and head into that strange place in physical being but only made brief psychic jaunts courtesy of something like an internet. They were safe this way and this was how they would raise their children. They were sometimes worried about juvenile misbehaviour, about youth culture disrespecting verities of their elders, about infiltration of proscribed substances, or devices, or thought. They allowed themselves to worry about the state of the world only when that world was the Reserve and others like it. They allowed regression in many social interactions, a rise in territorial disputes with near Cities or even a few other near Reserves, a dispute about how rational or alarmist were the True Humans, moderate in their Reserve but said to be fanatical in this other place. They told themselves that they were not such dangerous atavists, that such movements would not infest their sober community. They debated the probability of mass human movements always coming to grief, and how best to avoid collateral damage. They often had relatives or friends on other reserves, with whom the Internet was occasionally opened, and proclaimed how open the world was, even when such community was virtually identical and only a time zone away. They talked of how there would be a student exchange next season, how youth visiting and youth visitors would inject energy and hope and a sense of how this world persists as human, even with the aliens. They were able sometimes to talk of their own youthful travels, to talk of a time before terrorism security degraded Europe into an armed prison for its populace, before the disrupting wars tore Africa to pieces, before drone wars, robot wars, all the wars nobody would allow themselves to remember. They thanked the advent of the aliens for the end of that senseless slaughter. They sometimes had to listen to someone launching into futile verbal attack on the aliens, claiming we were doing fine, we were reaching world peace, we were no longer poisoning the world or causing the oceans to rise, we were learning to love rather than fight each other, we were devising new technologies to feed, to clothe, to shelter, to reach to the future. They sometimes listened politely to the rant, they sometimes took leave, they sometimes decided it was his house so you had to listen. They mostly agreed that this was overstating the case, rather that the aliens had been beneficial, that had the advent not come who knew what horrors our world would have become. They decided it was the shot speaking, and even the speaker would not remember what he had said by tomorrow. They laughed understandingly as they wobbled to their vehicles, looked back and hoped the children upstairs had not heard the rant, left the argument behind and forgotten.

RESET

When the aliens came it was not how we expected. We thought they would come in some recognizable interstellar form, in craft of some sort, powered by alien technology far in advance. We had expected physical manifestation. We had expected the physical presence of immense interstellar spaceships hovering over our major cities or rising behind the far side of the moon, or flotillas of armed spacecraft hurtling through our atmosphere to devastate airfields or aircraft carriers caught with squadrons of fighter jets on the ground. We had seen the movies. We had expected hailing or surprise attack. We had expected message or demand. We did not expect aliens to come in such an alien manner, but of course how could we know how aliens would come. We would not be ignored. We did not even know how to say how they came because the objective universe did not change, at first. We had the mistaken prejudice of our species that there was this objective universe that we could find again and the tilted inhumanity of our advent with the aliens, the emptiness, the fullness, the terror and the mourning for all that was human, would be survived into something we called objective. Some people knew this was not the situation. Some people withdrew. Some people scrambled to be more present than ever, and as it is always easier to destroy than create, as the wondrous exhilaration of destruction is more human than the gradual and unknowable majesty of creation, there were orgies of such hatred released by some of our humans. Some people would preemptively attack the aliens but this was avoided because of fear of whatever great armament they might introduce and destroy us, so as always humans fought humans. Some people launched abortive campaigns of destruction, of coups and revolutions, as if this mattered more than simply insisting your own power by slaughtering other humans, but these actions quickly collapsed when it was clear nothing but bleak fear animated them. Some people thus rejected this nihilism and became fervent converts to newborn faiths. Some people enjoyed this nihilism, and so continued to kill in greater and greater numbers, but we appealed to the aliens and after some moments of contemplation, this and that person and followers were simply removed, erased, forgotten. Some people went for refuge to religions to ways of thought to this or that intoxicant or narcotic or hallucinogen. Some people even refused to believe in the aliens, though all your fellows, all your families, all your enemies, were united in affirmation. Some people in the first awareness of the advent would claim that the reality of the aliens was of no consequence, would say this, whether objective or subjective, was no answer to our human lives, our human histories, for it was now not that they came but how they came. Some people would say that the rules of our universe as revealed through centuries, through microseconds, through all our human sciences, these rules were yet unbroken. Some people insisted that our most brilliant understanding was that physical laws were like true spiritual laws without some enforcing authority, but those were only laws that could not be breached and that in some way the aliens had not disproved or destroyed but only evaded them. Some people went for scientific refuge in popularized theoretical books, convinced some human could explain how the aliens evaded them and came here. Some people went for refuge in science fiction or fantasy texts which had long refused reasoned limits of the physical universe, in which humans or aliens were in some way always transcending that universal speed limit of light in a vacuum, were always meeting, fighting or fucking aliens who were no stranger ultimately than the human models from which they were derived. Some people went for refuge in the nonsense sense of quantum physics that offered enough room for their imaginations, but actual theories of superstrings and other sub-subatomic concepts were often seen as equally works of fiction. Some people said there was only one universe. Some people said there were many universes. Some people spoke of warping space-time. Some people spoke of black holes disrupting our universe. Some people were convinced by something they called entanglement, where this object here was reproduced there with no apparent communication that would exceed the speed of light, but in our theory there would have to be a receiver as well as sender. Some people seized this limited understanding to explain how this group or that group were traitors to the human race, particularly scientists who were willing to speak, were open, were naïve. Some people who were never convinced by the project of human rationality said that obviously we had misunderstood or mistaken all those rules. Some people knew this argument was fruitless and knew we should simply await correction from these aliens. We learned from the aliens the technology we had to build to welcome their physical presence, but soon of course it was their psychological presence that had the greatest effect, soon we would see that however they came we could not resist or fight them. We built devices and instruments and tools according to their detailed plans, but these were needed only to then build the next generation of such devices and instruments and tools that would then build the next generation, and so on we continued. We did not fully understand what we were fashioning, not in theory, not in practice, but our engineers were pleased to see that magic of the alien technology was possible by extrapolation of generations of engineering. We thought at first that the aliens would find it best to allow us all to understand their tech, their theory, their magic, and so by reverse engineering we humans would become men like gods, like them. We were wrong.

REAL

She is the girl he loves. She is the girl, she is the woman, she is
the friend, she is more than a friend, she is the woman he loves,
and so in the many ways she is real if not actual, ideal if not
abstract. She is real in a virtual and not a possible way, not she
who lacks only to be possibly real, not she already existing but a
girl it seems he must create. She is ideal but not someone who
borrows this quality and that quality of any other girl or woman,
she is ideal in herself and not just real in the way so many others
describe, she is ideal but in this world, this creative world, this
world that precedes her. She is not an ideal form in which all
women he loves must participate, must manifest, must prove
someone before, someone who is only different in her reality
rather than ideal. She is the woman he loves. She is the woman
who loves him, she loved him then and will and does love him,
so it is not surprising she does not exist. She is not one woman
now or ever. She is the woman he loves, who is the girl he loves,
who is to say she loves him, who is not him, who would want her
to love him, who is to say she loves. She is the girl he loves. She
is the girl he hopes loves him. She is his first girlfriend from his
adolescence he can remember and from before he can remember.
She is real in the sense she has been in his thoughts and in his

desires since before he could even imagine her, before he knew any way to know her, before there was any way to know her. She is real in the sense that if there are two worlds, one of change and one of permanence, one of sensuous experience and one of rational contemplation, one of becoming and one of being, she precedes any sort of real and is more real than any of these. She is real and she is not real. She is the girl he loves. She is a girl he wants to know and wants to be with, just when he is twelve years, but already there are cliques forming, already he is falling naturally to the cadre of students with intellectual facility but no physical ability or aptitude, and so she is not among his friends, his nascent social world. She is not one of the girls who come to their after-school party, not one of the girls who are perhaps bright, not one of the girls who do like him, as he discovers after meeting the girls after the newspaper route of his friend, as he discovers or perhaps only confirms, as this friend decides to ask the girls who they like best out of the boys in their group, and after a brief conference he does not hear, they all say him. She is not one of these girls. She is perhaps whom he would say he loves, not these girls, not these girls who look at him expectantly, not these girls who ask for something he does not know, something such as his gratitude, his shyness, his response more than looking away, for he does not know what to say but only jerks the wagon now empty of newspapers, jerks the wagon on which three of the girls are perching, spilling them onto the gravel alleyway. She is not one of these girls. She comes from down the hill in the town class, the working class, the lower-income class, and perhaps he could have learned about her, perhaps if his questions continued she might have learned how he felt for her. She is the girl he loves but he sits behind her in the corner of the class and she never has a reason to look there. She is not tall, she is thin, she is small, she has no womanly shape, she has an oval-shaped face, she has pale blue eyes, she has pink lips, she has a shy smile that is never for him. She has all these qualities but it is her helmet of pale short blonde hair that he loves. She has no budding breasts and her legs are straight and neither thin nor fat. She is the first girl he remembers but not the first girl he does not remember. She is the first girl he can remember being so different from the ideals, not abstract as one or another boy shows one of those magazines of naked women. She is the girl he loves. She is not shaped whom any other boys should enjoy. She is not big-breasted. She is not narrow waist and wider hips. She is not elaborate long hair. She is not painted lips and blushing cheekbones. She is somehow more attractive than this to him, though she is also the first girl he feels his friends find ordinary. She is special, she is more than her look, she is more than her first boyfriend the star athlete, he wants to be hers, her to be his. She is not one of his natural cliques and has no reason to look to where he sits at the back of class. She is something more than his friends can imagine, so perfect, so special, so ideal, so real, that the boys he knows wonder if he wants something more than the usual feathered hair and flashing smile and wayward erect nipple on her swimsuit poster, but he is not aroused but embarrassed when one boy introduces him to a stack of pornographic magazines involving animals as well as naked women, magazines of his parents from Sweden. She is the girl he loves though he agrees without sincerity that this movie actor or that movie actor is beautiful. She is the girl he loves but that year ends and the next year she is not in his class, and the year after that he lives where his father is working on sabbatical, and the year after that they move to a new place just outside the city where he goes to a different school. She is the girl he loves but he no longer sees her every day and in time he thinks he should forget her. She is the girl he loves and he does not forget her. She is not the girl he knows when he is a freshman and his sister a junior at the high school in the islands when his father is working at another university. She is not these other girls who are cheerleaders who often occupy the swimming pool of the complex, who are dating athletes and big men on campus. Perhaps what he wants from her is the same care and closeness as once he had with his sister. She is not a cheerleader, who already knows to compliment strength or tallness or ability yet treat those athletic egos gently as little brothers. She is not in fact like any of his sister's friends for whom he does not exist in any way. She, his sister, is becoming a woman and this means becoming like all those girls he does not understand, becoming just a girl, any girl, and not someone who devises adventures, not someone who gives him any role. She, his sister, is not the girl he loves. She, his sister, introduces him sometimes, but they are never the girls whom he loves. She, not his sister, is the girl he loves but she does not exist. She is the girl he must make real in his love. She is the girl he loves but she is not in this new school and if he could, he would return to the city, return to the high school she would now be attending, return and confess or assert or proclaim his love for her. She is the girl who will be the woman he loves, and here in his loss she is the girl he loves, but he is always too late, too late in meeting, too late in recognizing her, too late in loving her. She is the girl he loves and perhaps it is as important as her pale blonde hair and her pale blue eyes, as important and as central to his yearning, that she has left, that in some or in many ways, he is always too late. She is the girl he loves though when he is young he does not know this different love, this desire for her to be near, this desire that is not the love he bears for his father, for his mother, for his sister. She does not look like these most important women in his life. She does not talk to him or show in so many ways that he is important to her, that she loves him. She is the girl who becomes the woman he loves but he is sceptical of words, he is unwilling to allow his articulate speech, his political speech, his moments of charm, to be true reflections of love. She is beyond words so he does not trust his failed conversations, his ease, his vocabulary, his pace, his wit to in any way express true reflections. She is the girl who becomes the woman he loves, but this is not clear, this is not the natural progression, not the natural maturity, for in some ways she never is more than a girl. She is not the ideal he can share with his friends and even some of the girls to whom he is a friend. She is always this arbitrary image, her pale blonde hair and her pale blue eyes, an obsession he would perhaps desire to leave behind, to move to adulthood, to become an adult, to understand that she is more than she looks. She is the girl he loves. She is the girl he must create that he loves. She becomes one of the first and certainly the first person he draws. She is always there, she is within his thoughts, she need never be a model, she need never be physically present, she dwells in his most remote and most immediate but most unknown part of his mind. She is the girl he loves even when he comes to recognize she is not the girl most of his friends love, just a girl, just a girl he could meet in halls at school, just a girl who is no more confident in being a focus of attraction than he is a focus of attraction to some girls. She is the girl he loves but soon she is the girl who is young, just a girl, just not in his year, just a subject of jeers from the boys, just noted as too girlish, too young, too flat-chested, too narrow-hipped. She is the girl he loves and momentarily he wonders if there is something wrong in him, but only for a moment, for he is attracted to a certain look but never truly to little girls. She is the girl he loves but not as a girl. She is the girl he loves but she is not the girl who loves you. She is the girl he loves but it is never those qualities as a person that matter, those qualities other women or girls will claim really matter. She is the girl he loves but at this age he does not think of relationships or conversations or interests as what truly matters. She is the girl he loves but not a puzzle to share with his friends, certainly not with his big sister, who has decided he is just a typical boy, a typical boy becoming a typical man, but he has a friend who is handsome and even as an adolescent is never without as girlfriend, who is handsome, who is confident, who is maybe even smart, but to him he is not interesting, and this must be the same puzzle girls see in beautiful but dull classmates. She is the girl he loves but like many other girls she wants the handsome boy. She is the girl he loves and there is no reasonable complaint, no surprise, for if he is so attracted to ephemeral surface, how can he expect her to be different. She is the girl he loves, she is this virtual, this ideal, this perfection if only to him. She is the girl he loves and for some reason or many reasons he feels he is not possibly the boy she could love. She is the girl he loves and never adjusts her presence in real girls he knows, in anyone real, in anyone even actors or singers or athletes, of whom he only by image knows. She is the girl he loves. She is then the friend of a girl whose mother cuts his hair, this mother who approves of her daughter, who approves of him for her daughter, whose daughter he does not want but her friend. She is the girl that he could perhaps come to know through this girl, but he is not yet careful in planning some way to come to know her. She is the girl he loves. She is not the girl who loves him, though perhaps that is overstating her interest, and when he talks to a boy he knows he offends him by not agreeing to how wonderful is this girl whose mother cuts his hair. She is not the girl he loves. She is not the girl he loves and only momentarily does he wonder if in fact he loves boys, but this is not a real question, not a real concern, for in creating this ideal fantasy it is always she from before he can remember. She is the girl he loves who does interest other boys in his adolescence, this interest that he feels he can never compete with, this interest that he shares only with graphite and white paper, this interest that precedes his adult recognition, this interest that finds him before he can remember drawing pictures of this blonde girl. She is the girl he loves to draw but this is not from a model and not from a photograph, and somehow she is always looking away, always turning her body away, always her unseen face looking somewhere that is only ever the blank of the paper. She is the image that comes to his thoughts but often he distrusts his desires and tries to draw other girls. She is the girl he loves and these other drawings, even from the fashion magazines of his sister, even girls from pornographic magazines as work for his friends, even all these other sources of beautiful images, are never the girl he loves. She is the girl he loves and never the real girls, the girls from school, the girls to whom he is one of the football players, the girls for whom this is status, though he only joins the team because his friends encourage him and not because of athletic ability and interest, though he is never skilled, there are real girls he could know. She is the girl he loves, he searches for everywhere. She is the girl he loves that he searches in all those large-format, often coffee-table, books of artists who should inspire him, of varied artistic lineage, of everything from da Vinci to Degas, but the nearest he comes then to visualizing his ideal is always Botticelli. She is the girl he loves who lived hundreds of years past and continues to live now in so many paintings. She is the girl he loves and for once it is her face he can see, for once she is not looking away, for once he can imagine her features in shadow and curve and almost tactile smoothness. She is the girl he loves, dancing in springtime or rising out of the sea on a seashell. She is so many girls in springtime, repeated images, repeated modelling, and for some reason he can only imagine that it is all images done at once, as if a photograph, as if he had found so many girls so beautiful, and only later that he will realize that as a painter it is always the same model. She is the girl he loves and later, years later, decades later, he will learn the name of the model, he will learn she was desired and ideal for those city princes who commissioned these works, he will learn she was only seventeen when she posed and two years later died, he will learn that even in this imaginary love he is too late, always too late. She is the girl he loves and now that he is old enough he has no difficulty and no guilt in purchasing all those magazines of naked women. She is the girl he loves but she is not the girl next door, she is not the girl seen through Vaseline, she is not the girl in any of the poses but in all, and he finds himself creating her out of the images he buys. She is not the girl he loves in these pictures, and he does not mutilate actual images, he does not cut the girls in pieces, he does not find her in abstract images, for somehow it is not separate elements that characterize her beauty but the integrated image. She is the girl he loves that is all these girls, all these images, and his creation is only in freeing the photos from unnecessary companions, other girls, other pictures, other texts, other ads, and creating pamphlets of this girl and that girl. She is the girl he loves. She is the girl he has combined in a sort of mental collage, not an actual work, not an actual perfection, for he knows the blank wall or the artwork not made actually exceeds whatever work he would place there or fashion out of fragments. She is the girl he loves and she is not in these magazines or in his obsessive work on these images. She is the girl he loves that he does not find in fragments, though he learns more here of abstraction in visual art than he ever does in Art classes at university. She is the girl he always sees in the same perspective, within possibility. She is not emulating great pleasure as she poses, she is not eyes closed in orgasmic oblivion, she is not displaying her cunt, she is not this picture where half is her anus and vulva which is by photographic perspective larger than her grin, her lost face, lost personality, though he will not agree that such images are by any theory rape. She is the girl he loves but she is never any of these images, no matter how he masturbates with them within reach, though his eyes are closed and it is only in his mind he sees her. She is the girl he loves. She is the girl he loves and does not see her in this way. She is the girl he loves and later, years later, decades later, there are always girls who will be flattered for him to draw them nude or even be photographed in any of these ways. She is the girl he loves but he is confused and even angry that her image should so continue to dominate, that there are other girls he must admit are beautiful, are desired by his friends, but he always returns to this one focus. She is the girl he loves and by chance he discovers her image in a girl he comes to know. She is the girl he loves such that he asks to draw her, first draw her from profile, then draw her from three quarters, then draw her from the right side looking up, then draw her from the left side looking down, then draw her from directly in front in muted light that does not disguise her pensive gaze, her occupied gaze, her pale blue eyes reading an art text, her questioning gaze that breaks into a smile when he shows what he drawn. She is the girl he loves and so he has rendered her beautiful in his way. She has short blonde hair brushed from a centre part, she has a strong forehead, she has big eyes, she has a button nose, she has lips he wants to kiss even as he first sees her. She is the girl he loves who is a year older in the shared drawing class at university. She has short blonde hair, she has pale blue eyes, she is almost his height, she is thin, she has neither breasts nor hips of usual girls, but the key is that she is an artist. She is the girl he loves, who loves the same way of being in the world, by being an artist. She shares hours looking at Art books, texts for class, shows at museums, and they can actually argue about this work or that artist, she can proclaim Miro the greatest that week and then Schiele the greatest the next week, she can reject his fascination with Stella and Johns, and they can argue with passion and seriousness but they are at least in the same world. She is a year older and he mistakenly imagines she will know more than he how to satisfy their shared desires. She is the girl he loves. She is the girl he loves who does not impress his friends for she is not their beautiful swimsuit issue model. She is the girl he loves but to these friends she is not sexy, she is too tall, she is too thin, she is sexy to him, too sexy, a question he can never explain. She is not a fashion model though perhaps could be. She is the girl he loves who does impress the other girls he knows, who imagine he must be deeper and more impressed by real qualities of person rather than just looks. She is the girl he loves but much of that is virtual attraction. She is the girl he loves not as embodiment of the possible but presence of the virtual, she is not some possibility of what he loves granted the addition of being real here and now, she is the virtual ideal made present, though at this time he is not yet nineteen and the distinction is not clear. She is the girl he loves but not the mother who loves him for her. She is the girl he loves who does not tell him of her problems at home, of how seriously they argue, of how her mother threatens to kick her out, of all this, of any of this. She is the girl he loves and with whom he first has adult sex, real sex, the kind of sex his friends had imagined to be the real reason to be with a girl, to be the real reason the mother of this girlfriend would kick her out. She is the girl he loves who mistakenly believes he should know what he is doing, that he must be experienced, that as he is knowledgeable in many ways there is no doubt he would be knowledgeable in this way. She is the girl he loves but he is unable to admit this is all new also to him. She is the girl he loves and later, years later, decades later, he will wish he had known more and now does know more and as with anything, practice improves practice. She is the girl with whom the inside of the car becomes familiar in the way wherever one has sex or works becomes more real when you have sex there, and so his room at home when they are alone there, or her room at home when they are alone there, or this empty Art classroom at the University, or this place far beyond the squash courts at the University, or this place where the stairs end at a landing no one goes to. She is the girl he loves and it is first she who rejects him, she who tells him they have to stop because of her mother, she who hurts him in this way, then it is she who comes to him two weeks later and wants to continue in private just for sex, and so all these other places become familiar. She is the girl he loves and the way this will become does not at first bother him. She is the girl he loves and he can bring other girls by, flirt with other girls, be with other girls, and she can do nothing. She is the girl he loves who finds him in an empty art classroom talking to a girl who actually would impress his male friends, a girl who does not attract him though she should, but he wants the tears later from the girl he loves when she tells him she is sorry to have interrupted something. She is the girl he loves. She is the reason he begins to skip class and projects and finally leave school. She is the girl he loves and she is the girl who says she loves him, she is the girl, she is always the girl, and it is she who ends this private sex, perhaps she wants more than sex, perhaps she wants better sex, and it is only through a young student who knows them both that he learns she will marry this other man. She is the girl he loves and after her there are other girls but there are no perfect combinations of physical attraction and artistic obsession, though he never tells other girls this, never more than gestures to her work, her pictures, her history, for this time is past and this affair is over, though it is only later, years later, decades later, that he will admit to anyone their private afternoons. She is the girl he loves but could never love enough. She is the girl he loves but as always, somehow he is too late. She is the girl he loves who only confirms his personal certainty that he is not to be loved, that he lacks some quality that summons love from a girl, though his big sister only shrugs it off, though she knows it is only momentary, though she knows his charms are enough for more women than he imagines. She is the girl he loves but when he is free of all attachments he does not rush to recreate that lover. She is the girl he loves. She is the girl he loves and it is not too much a surprise that he loses her. She is the girl he loves and he is never more than a boy who loves her. She is the girl he loves but this has become an obsession image no other will ever come close to, not this actual girl, not this girl he knew in those private places, for she was only his failed attempt to create the girl he loves. She is the girl he loves but it is only his dream, his virtual, and he is always too late. She is the girl he loves who is first a friend, who says she loves him, who says this before he says he loves her, but this is a different love from his mother or big sister. She is the girl he loves after she says this because he wants so much to believe this. She is the girl he loves that he meets through a social club at University, where she is not the first woman to say he should become a psychiatrist, that he seems kind, that he seems perceptive, that he seems like someone to whom she could talk, she could confess, she would listen to. She is the girl he loves but he knows it is said that he who psychoanalyzes himself has a fool for a patient, and he feels need for someone to explain himself to himself, before he would venture to help another on that invisible but important psychic landscape. She is a girl who he imagines in previous centuries would encourage him to become a priest. She is the girl he loves who tells him he should become a politician, at first this is a compliment but eventually as they live together she will accuse him of his facility with words that never truly answer questions asked, she will accuse him of being manipulative, she will accuse him of being insincere. She is the girl who knew the girl he had loved in that private way but does not judge, does not excuse them, does not accuse them, does not wonder if he still has feelings for her, but only after months is she convinced and by that time the other has left for marriage and left for another city. She is the girl he loves first as a friend and then as a lover with no awkward time in between, only love as something to fall into, something he did not search for, something he does not name as love even after living with her for months. She is the girl he loves and she loves that he is an artist though for some reason he draws images not from models, not from landscapes, not something anyone else can see but images in his mind. She is the girl he loves, she is the girl he should love, for she is smart and she is kind and she is pleasant to look at, but she also knows she is not blonde enough or thin enough or tall enough in comparison to the other girl. She is attractive enough to be a part-time model, she is young enough that this is pleasing, she is young enough this pleases him as well, but mostly she is a physics student at university and so admires his father as a man who knows the joy of finding things out, and so admires his mother who is calm and makes everything possible for his father, and in turn his mother will wish that he will marry her. She is the girl he loves and they are the same age within a week, they are twenty-one when they begin to live together. She is the girl he loves and is comfortable with the apprehension that he is first and finally attracted to the way she looks. But this is never the truth, never the fact of friendship, never the passivity with which he accepts her love, never the fact he must leave home and she will take him in. She is able to work hard and perhaps it is this that allows his parents to pay for his rent and she is not punished for loving him. She and he find a new apartment within walking distance to class but they are some distance from the grocers and then his parents give him one of the family cars, the one he is always using anyway, the one he needs to drive them around the city, though she continues to walk to class and he uses this transport to free them from the local grocery store, the ordinary grocery store, and they now visit a few Italian grocers who are on the other side of the city. She is the girl he loves and she has become something like a project shared, desires shared, possibilities shared, as they learn to cook first Italian then Mexican dishes, as they learn to plan menus and alter recipes with lower amounts of fat, for they both want to be thin. She wants to be thin as a model and he wants to be thin to please her and she wants to be thin to please him. She comes with him to his parents' place just outside the city, where they do their laundry and cook dinner and visit and this seems like a mature love, a working love, a shared love, and though his parents do not understand his desire to be a visual artist, they trust her and it seems she understands. She is the woman he loves and he would like to draw something or paint something that would please her, nothing too abstract for her, nothing too realistic, nothing she can explain in words, and this is how they first came together, with him talking about art, him breaking art down, him telling her sincerely that he believes art must appeal to the viewer before all the other theoretical assertions, and she would listen innocent and convinced by this passion. She tells him she wants to look like this model or like that model but these are slick professional photographs, she tells him this, she wonders if this can ever be art, she listens and he listens and soon it is too clear they both want the same thing. She looks at his work but there is no object to which it can be compared. She looks at his work and asks why he never draws from life and he must say he does not create images of the beautiful visible but creates the invisible beautiful. She listens to him speak but truly if he could tell her in words what he is trying for, he would not try so hard to create what words can never say. She listens to him and imagines even that he will succeed in some time soon, for it is clear how passionate his desires are and the world will not be so cruel to deny him. She is the girl he loves who never tells him he should use her as a model for is that not tradition for artists to use girlfriends or women they know to be subjects, but there is something he is not saying by never asking her to pose, there is something wrong with her she thinks, there is something wrong for all these months then years they are together. She is the woman he loves and so he comes to understand what she wants in how she lingers at his side as he draws spaceships and aliens and perhaps in coming years he could become a comic book artist. She is the girl he loves so he asks to draw her, first draw her from profile, then draw her from three quarters, then draw her from the right side looking up, then draw her from the left side looking down, then draw her from directly in front in muted light. She is the girl he loves but he is never happy with the images he draws of her. She is the girl he loves but she is not the girl he loves, for she is real, she is here and she is subtly different from the image that persists in his mind. She is the girl he loves but already he is too late. She is the girl he loves but she is not the girl he loves. She is the girl he loves but it is only reasonable for her to question his work, which is coming less and less, which is coming without his passionate evolution of style, which is now becoming further and further abstract and unapproachable. She is the girl he loves who comes across drawings from before of the other girl, who comes across him looking at the other girl, who comes to the only answer to his growing remoteness, who comes to believe it is this other woman he is looking for, when it is always the girl he loves that he searches for in all the work ever done and all the girls he has ever known. She is the girl he loves but she is not the girl he loves. She is the girl he loves and the girl he leaves for that other city, in order to become an artist, somehow. She is the girl he loves who remembers him and stays in contact with his mother. She is the girl he loves who hears two years later from his mother that he is in a coma, she hears this from the woman who had hoped to be her mother-in law, she hears this and the miles of telephone wire between them do not diminish her tears.

RESERVE

When they first came to be on the Reserve it did not seem too different from how things had always been. They had money of a kind, or at least numbers on account, and though it was useful only on the Reserve and a few other reserves, it did establish necessary stratification of society, the comforting sense you shared the world and wealth in understandable groups. They had money and even if the circuit of power was limited there was clear power and status amongst fellow humans, and no one cared too much what the rare visitor from the Cities thought of the traditional human technology and thinking, quietly incorporating only a few arbitrary improvements from the aliens. They saw now that the greatest and most useless driver for technological advance in the demands of our human, misnamed 'defence' industry was only gradually replaced by a desire to mimic the aliens. They did not say this aloud, and would sensibly never regret we humans no longer prosecuted wars, but there were arguments about how we humans could support our groups, how we could hold together, how we could admire our people and detest those others. They could not expect help from the aliens. They knew they were not all artists and even the grouped craftsman who helped fashion such works of collaborative arts, the seventh art, the cinema, were only a fraction of the populace in many Reserves. They had heard of those nodes where it seemed everyone was involved in art production, and not surprisingly many youth were often fleeing the comfort and stability of the Reserve for these places, the deserts, the mountains, the forests, the communes, the cities that were not the City. They lost many of the young generation, it was said, because somehow despite rigid censoring, the young were learning history, learning there was a place where to be different, to create, was honoured, not subject to the social pressure to offer only pleasant folktales for the Reserve. They might have wanted to censor any works of art or history from before the advent, but this was difficult to judge. They did not want to close down all aspects but only promote those aspects of the arts that demonstrated contemporary life was the best society humans had ever known. They did not add that the aliens had facilitated this but did not refuse this. They were not and would never agree with those who claimed species allegiance, those True Humans. They had some voices who argued that children and then youth should have complete freedom of cultural sources, should have art, should have history, should even come to visit the Cities, and in this way their judgment would be informed and they would obviously know the Reserve was the best society humans had ever known. They had these voices but such were quite regularly shouted down and never reached such power to implement such dangerous ideas. They said that the aliens knew best after all, that this was not stagnation, not surveillance, not censorship, but this was the way to live. They said it was as the Reserve Agent said in answering any crisis, that humans only now knew best how humans should live. They said the truth of our world could be compared to the history in books of the rarely visited library. They said there was freedom but not freedom to harm oneself. They said that one only had to look around to our safe and civilized communities and compare this to the strife, the madness, the violence we saw regularly through our far-seeing technologies, and that it was risible conspiracy theory that claimed we only saw what the aliens wanted us to see. They showed us what we needed to see. They showed us the other world, where humans still rejected gifts of the aliens or misapplied given technology in typical human perversion. They said that the psychological techniques used by the aliens to pacify humans and render them satisfied in stressful moments, their kind of gentle calmness that drew out our positive human qualities, were even used by humans in this or that City to convince the human populace that they flourished in the most degraded circumstances. They claimed the rest of the world envied the security and wealth of this Reserve, that it was the best Reserve, that our sports teams showed what humans could do with other humans. They said that art was essentially untrustworthy and too often seduced by the glamour of the Cities, that art was too often shiny vehicles for the worst ideological histories of humans before the advent. They said the answer was sport culture. They said it was easily understood and played out narratives that were even more pure in all their rules and determinations. They said it reflected the essence and truth of the human world. They said there were winners and losers. They said it made possible regular moments of emotional expression, but in its spontaneous generation no one could be certain it would be joy or sorrow, and then again there was another game in a few days, in months, in seasons, and it was entirely possible to become a fanatic for your team, to narrow meaning and value from the world, from the Reserve even, down to however long the game lasted. They said this was not meaningless but in fact the truest expression of our human being. They said proof of this was that the aliens did not seem to care. They said that the aliens did not play, did not understand the joy of such behaviour, so could not recognize the joy of leaving yourself and following the sense of this or that player or team.

They were briefly proud to be human. They organized competitions within the Reserve and with other Reserves. They adhered to rigorous testing against all sorts of performance-enhancing drugs, for the world might be unfair, but the sport must be fair.

RESET

When the aliens came it was not when we expected. We did not even know when they arrived, and once we knew, if ever we could have responded, it was too late. We were later told that they would not have come, they would not have contacted us if we had refused them, but we could not have refused what we did not know. We were not simply another species or another culture or another genome or another existential alien to be absorbed. We had seen the movies. We were different. We were not whales or dolphins or ants. We thought this made a difference to how the aliens would treat us and what would happen, though of course we humans were an elaboration of sentient terrestrial species, though of course we were capable intelligent animals, we were still all in all terrestrial and in many ways an inferior species that had dominated an inferior global evolution. We were nothing more than evolved intelligent apes of the same derivation as ancestors to those less intelligent apes currently dying out, their environments becoming ours as our world was becoming an extension of environments for the aliens. We argued to ourselves that we were more, but such contention required faith, required belief, required metaphysics of something like souls and some hopeful ethical framework to an indifferent universe. We had now lost any confidence that we were more than irrelevant background natives when the aliens came. We had now lost any practical certainty when the aliens came. We allowed ourselves to imagine there was some indefinable human quality that justified our being however that being was different from the aliens. We allowed ourselves to imagine that it was our jumble of individuals and groups, our 'I' and 'We' as much as 'They', that were useful strategies of sense and thought that the aliens wanted. We allowed ourselves to imagine that there was this undefined 'nature' of humans, some quality impossible to simulate and maybe for this reason not existing, or maybe something the aliens had lost, but there was and is no 'human nature'. We allowed ourselves to imagine we had aptitudes and possibilities and actions and thoughts. We allowed ourselves to imagine we had an entire spectrum of thought, but this was a misapprehension, a mischaracterization of what we humans had previously shared. We had no more than a human 'condition' in common, and when the aliens came that was all changed. We were all born and were old enough to die from the first breath. We feared and distracted ourselves from imminent end. We ignored and abstractly honoured our births. We moved our corpse only in one direction in time of various durations, yet our consciousness moved in all directions, unifying through realms we called now and past and present, and thought the time past was unalterable, the time future undetermined, the time present unknowable. We thought we shared this passage through time with each other and the world around us and of course the aliens. We were not wrong but not exactly right. We were all human when they arrived, but humans of differing ages, different maturity, and so when the aliens came this meant different things. We who were old were easily convinced that we humans were over, were meaningless, were no longer if ever had been something like the peak of an evolutionary tree. We were correctly reminded this was a mistake in thought, for we were no tree of definite peak from definite roots, we were not even a bush but some sort of groundcover rhizome with no peak, no special branches, no order, no single roots, that had momentarily been best adapted to conditions of our environment. We were reminded there had been discovered fossil remains, hip bones, femurs, skulls, toes, hands of other hominids who had lived contemporaneous with our ancestors, other hominids who died out or were absorbed into triumphant Homo sapiens. We could wonder how or why they had died but most everyone was convinced this was for the best, though it did not matter to those deluded souls who would refuse the concept of evolution, and anyway this was evolution from a completely alien power. We had been on the verge of becoming immortal, we thought. We were leaving our home planet, we were evading whatever destruction of our original cradle, destruction by rogue meteor or portended ecological collapse. We were too many, we were too valuable, at least to ourselves and by logical extension to the aliens. We knew our God or gods or the universe or the alien universe had some kind of purpose for us. We thought we were ready to evolve, not that so many of us as a species would have no future. We who were old were soon aware we were over as a species. We who were young had no such loyalty to what-ever we had been when the aliens came. We thought our elders were mistaken, were simply too limited by what we had been to imagine what we would be. We might have been sad for them but mostly we ignored them. We knew they had nothing to tell us. We were on to the further adventures of our lives. We thought the aliens were here to aid us to become more than human, to end our protracted childhood and introduce us to the universe, and the pathetic fear of the concept of the last man was no more than the fear of a child who wonders where the light goes when we switch the power off. We would become everything and more and suffered no paranoid delusions and fears of the aliens. We did not fear invasion or extinction, perhaps because we were already invaded in our minds when the aliens came, perhaps we knew we humans were then immediately extinct anyway. We wanted this great adventure. We were wrong.

REAL

He is the man who does not exist. He is the son of the man who knows the joy of finding things out, he is the son of the woman who is calm, he is the brother of the elder sister who has always done the right thing. He is this man and he does not exist. He is not the man who writes this narrative. He is nothing more than another character whom no one will say is real, no matter how accurately this work is autobiographical, no matter how this character persists in this voice and who would like to convince, who needs to convince, who pretends to no other purpose, that he exists. He is the man who does not exist and a man who not does exist, he is the man who does exist and does exist, he is the man who neither exists nor not exists, he is the man who both exists and does not exist. I offer this not as alien logic but in opposition to the binary and exclusive logic common to introductory Western philosophy, this idea that any proposition is true or false and nothing in between and never both, this four limbs of Buddhist logic. He is the man who survives the coma, almost entirely whole, that is his cognitive functions of logic, of thought, of ability to work with information in a meaningful way, of applying gained information, of performing preferential changes, of ability to change beliefs of information, all these functions resident in the frontal lobe, all these functions appear undamaged to any great degree, all these functions associated with abstraction, learning, intelligence, mind, all these characteristics by which other people might identify him, all these aspects survive intact the brain injury and subsequent coma. He is the man who survives the coma, almost entirely whole, that is his memory functions of sensory memory, of short-term memory, of long-term memory, of the sort episodic, of the sort semantic, of the sort procedural, then of recalling memory, of forming memory, of planning and evaluating outcomes of this or of that behaviour, of speaking and of hearing, of social awareness and of empathy, of what humans usually call personality, all these aspects survive intact the brain injury and subsequent coma. He is the man whose memory remembers often too clearly the man he was before the coma, too clearly the man he was that is not revealed in systematic scientific measures, too clearly the man who is lost irrecoverable now, too clearly the man who was young and unformed and there are no arguments essayed and there are no assertions declared, too clearly this man no longer exists. He is the man who does not exist and must exist and will exist, the man who decides his person is performance more clearly than ever before, the man who decides the man does not exist, the man who decides how in each way he will now exist. He changes his name the way he had always wanted but never had the excuse to do so, he changes his birthday but this is only momentary and the woman who is calm refuses this strategy as no more than a desire for more birthday presents. He is damaged in his brainstem near the upper end of his spinal column and none or little of that typically human forebrain is recognizably damaged. He retains memory and retains language. He retains more language centres on the left frontal lobe, he retains more spatial centres on the right lobe to tell where and at what orientation his body exists, where and how surrounding objects exist, he retains flexibility of thought patterns to solve problems, retains ability to use input from the environment to guide learning. He is the man whose temporal lobes to the back and outside and beneath the frontal and parietal lobes appear undamaged or strangely damaged, for though speaking and hearing interpretation, of memory and identifying objects, of recognition of faces and scenery, of smells and of sounds, are still resident, for some reason no one knows he now speaks with a thick English-sounding accent, but he can make himself easily heard, make himself understood, for there is no slurring or odd emphasis to the clarity of this voice, this voice he does not even hear from inside and it is not until he hears his voice on an answering machine that he will learn he speaks this way. He is a closed-head injury, where the injured brain tissue is caused not by objects violently introduced, but by impact of the brain against the skull. He appears at first entirely whole unless the patch over the left eye is noted, he appears able but for the wheelchair, for no one can see the hearing deficit, no one can hear the speaking deficit, no one can know any memory or thought damages. He has unknown damages or deficits that no one can be certain of until he is awake, until he can answer probing questions he must always answer on a sliding scale from yes always to maybe sometimes to no never, until he can become aware and accept his losses. His doctors and therapists and nurses are professionally cautious, for in this way he has a lucky coma, he has a coma that could by mere location of injury render him blind or unable to walk or unable to think. He is a lucky man. His occipital lobe is the last and possibly worst to be damaged, for it is here he has processing of visual information, here he has discrimination of movement, he has discrimination of colour, he has recognition and refusal to understand the deficit of misidentifying objects. He knows there is something else lost but no one will understand why sometimes he would rather be blind, rather be in a wheelchair, rather be anything than this, for the injury has lost him that trait once meaning more to him, that trait he identified with, that trait that described everything of that man who does not exist. He knows it is others who will make the final determination in one obvious way, yet he also knows he knows he is what he had always known, and never known and never could know, and both knows and does not know, but the trait of being an artist is not at this age something he will understand philosophically. He is an artist. He has lost certain physical skills but has not lost whatever constellation of brain aptitude or deficit that enables or curses the artist. He is already telling himself that as he was not expressing himself in an entirely physical way, as a physical artist, a dancer or an athlete, but perhaps as a visual artist, he will learn something about art, this injury will strip the inessential aspects of him, the accidental, the ephemeral aspects of his way of living, and reveal what it is in his art. He is telling himself this comforting tale in order to evade any sort of serious idea or repercussion of this injury. He is telling himself as he will tell others, and in this way is not accepting his losses, his injury, even the lost time, the unremembered lost time of the coma. He is not accepting his injury, some therapists, some people, some friends will accuse him, and all he can do is shrug. He does not cry. He does not dwell. He does not talk about it. He distracts himself. He thinks of women, who often enough seem curious, seem aroused, seem eager to help him forget the injury by whatever temporary expedience. He is relieved, that when the situation arises, so does he. He is surprised and not surprised that the President, the most powerful person in the most powerful country in the world, could throw away all dignity for a few moments of pleasure, when the girls he loves are not averse to this aspect of sex, when the girl he loves is eager, is pleased, is generally flattered to have such control. He is surprised but not surprised that the girl he loves is always interested, he is surprised and not surprised that his own obsessive type is still there, still possible, still interested in him. He is surprised and not surprised he can encourage one nurse to give him a manual job, another to give him a brief oral job, but this is never enough, this knowing he can receive pleasure, this knowing he is responsive, this knowing his brain injury does not affect him here. He wants to know if he can please the girl he loves. He wants to know if he can still attract the girl he loves, he can still please the girl he loves, he wants to know, he wants to know in the only way he can know, and so it is that he presses friendship and dignity for a few moments of pleasure. He loses her as a friend. He does not have a friend with whom he can share these concerns, he does not have the girl he loves, he has a girl he could love eagerly perform oral sex on him, but this is exactly as she does, no more than performance, no more indication of anything more, for no, she does not love him. He is surprised and not surprised that with this girl he can talk about other girls as she can talk about other boys in an entirely dispassionate way, and decides this is probably possible because they are no more than sex, because she wants one thing and he wants one thing, and there are no emotions interfering. He is pleased to find this out. He is surprised and not surprised later discovering her assertion that he doubtless can seduce women on the phone even as in turn he can hear little of her seducing him. He is surprised and not surprised that there is this thing known as bad sex, when he had tended to believe that sex was without qualifications, that sex was always good for him, that sex was never anything less, that sex must be practised as any physical action to learn what you practise. He is surprised and not surprised that there are girls he wants who do not want him, and girls who want him he does not want. He knows it is not merely the time in the coma that has affected an entire change of expectations and behaviour, but that the injury has subtly affected his social behaviour, his recognition of usual manners, usual limits, usual relations. He is surprised and not surprised that girls he does not know are so impressed he manifests no bitterness, no pity, no anger for the injury he has suffered. He shrugs. He will explain heartily and dismissively to the curious and the politely inquisitive that whereas for a quadriplegic none of the limbs are responsive to the brain, for a paraplegic only the lower body and legs are unresponsive, for him, he is a hemiplegic and it is as though he is divided right down the middle and one side of his body is as coordinated as ever and the other side is damaged if not immobile. He will tell the curious and the politely inquisitive that he is fortunate even in this injury for he does learn to walk again and such sufferers are often trapped in a wheelchair, such sufferers are often severely limited in articulation of speech, such sufferers are insensate on the injured side. He will tell people it is fortunate he survived the coma of forty-nine days with such limited deficits and really, other coma patients are worse off, other patients are limited to wheelchairs, other patients have sensory or cognitive or memory or all three combined deficits, others suffer, others deserve pity, others have lost far more than he. He is damaged on the left side of his brain, thus the right side of the body, and though his eyes can be operated on to bring the muscles to present their foci within five degrees vertical difference, though his hearing remains intransigent on the phone or when the other's face is not seen, he can hear in most conversations if not in groups, though he can learn to walk with a cane in his left hand but of course can never run or leap or even move fast, though in these many ways his survival is remarkably good, there is only the one thing, the minor thing, the little thing, that ensures he is the man who is dead. His right side includes his right hand and his right hand will now never handwrite or draw or paint or anything requiring artistic connection between hand and brain. He knows this deficit from the first moment he comes out of the coma. He knows this deficit as he tries to learn to write with his right hand, tries to record his memories of books he has read, tries to record memories of food he knows how to cook, tries to record memories of music he has listened to, tries to record memories of movies he has seen, tries to record memories of artwork he has seen, tries to record memories of plays he has seen or read. He knows this deficit that is impossible for him to imagine, though he remembers art class where students were directed to draw with the other hand, though he remembers the comic results, though that aspect of his mind which he identifies as himself, that aspect, that aptitude, that awkward blessing or curse, that urge to know the world through personally rendered images, has not been damaged, though it only took about twenty years' practice with his right hand which had the aptitude, to learn to forge some connection between image in his mind and image through his hand to the image on the paper. He has lost this ability. He is the man who does not exist. He will tell the man who knows the joy of finding things out but the only response is that he must find a new medium, that he must try drawing on a computer, that he must try drawing with the shapes graphic programs offer, that he must admit it was never the notation or line or style, but the subject was defined by composition and so how has he lost this, that anyway his father has lived his entire life without such artistic urges, that perhaps maybe of course his sisters are artists and it may be they can understand. He does not ask his aunts, for whatever skill he had as an artist was so radically different from either aunt that he fears their educated artistic rejection. He remembers the man he was before the coma too clearly. He remembers there once was the possibility of becoming an architect like his mother's father. He remembers he once had dreams he would call architectural, dreams in which he designed buildings that he tried to record upon waking, dreams which created buildings like mazes, dreams which created buildings that could never be realized either in design or materials, dreams which created buildings that were in some way never fortresses but always bridges. He remembers a city library designed like a giant cylinder with radiating shelves within, with public spaces arrayed like the panopticon once designed for prisons, but these were no prisons, these were all books and books promise freedom in space and time, but he did not become an architect and only now does he realize as architect how severe could have been the loss of coordination for drawing. He remembers with regret all those works he never pursued and now never will. He is not that man, he tells himself again and again. He is a man who does not exist. He must go forward, he must understand that was another life, he must work with the limitations, he must be pragmatic, he must recognize the possible, these are the contentions he must allow himself to act on, but for him it is not politics, not the art of the possible, for him it is art and all art is of the impossible. He desperately throws himself into the process of rehabilitation and it is only through these months these years that he realizes the simple truth that informs even this apparently simple act of walking, the simple truth that informs even memories of that man who does not exist, the simple truth that you learn what you practise, the simple truth that in many ways belongs only to memory of that man who does not exist, the simple truth that reminds him of the friend girl on the high school basketball team who in great annoyance told him the main reason he was not improving as an athlete on the boys' high school football team was that he did not practise. The man who does not exist persists in body at least, and with this persists in attitude, in what he will decide is the curse of perfectionism, this urge to walk perfectly, this anxiety of walking anything less than as described, when his first and last physical therapists will insist that in fact no one walks perfectly, that people walk from A to B on the shortest route by habit unthinking, for it is not true that when a thing is worth doing a thing is worth doing right when the truth is when a thing is worth doing it is a thing worth doing. He is a man who does not exist, but even in this case he would like to not exist completely, when it is unfortunate but unavoidable that his body remains the same, when it is his body that refuses to listen to his injured brain, when it is his body that floats in imagination, slightly imbalanced as a homunculus in his thought, as if the body is not throughout the brain. He is a man who does not exist and may never have existed, for whom he was for others is not whom he was for himself. He was thought an artist who evidently ingested significant quantities of some drugs, to explain the elaborate sketches of spacecraft and aliens and robots somewhat like those artists of the movie with that effective chest-buster scene, drugs had to be the reason, somehow this argument had more force than that he drew on science fiction and even fantasy as sources, and surely not all of those artists were on drugs of some sort. He had decided these images had overstayed their welcome and that the work of his favourite artists was in fact almost entirely of the representational sort even how invented was the subject. He was thought an artist though this was more likely an appraisal from those who were not artists, or who considered illustration of imagined subjects, always heavily inclusive of spacecraft and aliens and robots, as the most exceptional work. He was thought an artist though he did not trust his art. He is a man who does not exist. He is thought a smart kid but never feels comfortable amongst peers for whom intellect is a major definition of self. He is a smart kid who stays up too late on weeknights and sleeps through Math or Physics or both. He is certain he is an artist so feels he does not need math or physics or both. He is a man who does not exist. He can no longer demonstrate much physical dexterity, in running, in leaping, in hitting, or even the more sedentary sort of coordination such as required for manual tasks with his right hand, manual tasks he had obsessively practised, manual tasks that allowed him some representational facility, detail, shading, contours, and smooth or deliberately rough lines. He knows that these are for most people in his situation minor deficits, for most people of little loss considering the fatal possibilities or considering the severity of possibilities, so he deliberately decides to ignore these losses. He tries for months of his rehabilitation to recover his handwriting with his right hand, but it does not move fluidly, or move rigidly, move repetitively the same lines, the same curves, the same size, though it is recognizable as his own, and the writing he had once decided looked as though he was mechanical, as though printing now has default personality, now is not printing and precise but rather wildly uneven. He believes that if he can just recover his handwriting, his artistic skill will also recover, but it is only after consulting his physical therapists, he learns that no one knows how much will return, as the gradient of physical recovery that had been so steep in the first days, first weeks, first months, will become closer and closer to a horizontal line and will never be, never, complete recovery. He learns that his fine motor skills will never increase in pace either, his fine motor skills remain incapable of following that line in his mind, his fine motor skills must be replaced by digital skills, such as he may now write on the computer by hitting the relevant keys, such a pace that outstrips the usual hunt-and-peck technique, for he had taken typing one year in high school and the placement of keys, the correct digit to use on hitting, remains remarkably intact. He can only rely on his left hand for this skill, as the right is too slow, too inaccurate, too wandering. He writes only his signature with his left hand if he can avoid all other times people write, for though it is primarily the slow pace which bothers him, there are other difficulties, such as size or space or lines or horizontal angle, that are also constant, also erroneous, though he discovers that if he looks at his writing later, if neither he nor anyone else had watched the writing, his script is not uniquely difficult. He recalls once the present from the younger of his father's sisters, the visual artist who had heard he liked to write, of a calligraphy set, of pen and ink with several nibs, with ink reservoir, with a brief instruction guide, with hopes he would use them. He never had. His aunt had once helped him with shading a face to give it more shape, more dimension, and later seeing his felt pen sketches suggested he learn drypoint as it was clear his eye saw in lines, in contours, in sharply edged compositions. He remembers her advice that one summer she had visited, advice as an artist, advice his father never knew to offer, advice his mother would say came only from his father's side of the family. He had developed through the years intent towards representational facility rather than expressive notation, towards something similar to what he saw, rarely obviously what he felt, even when what he saw were those familiar spacecraft and aliens and robots. He remembers once in high school art class a project in which the student was encouraged to tell a story in images, in sequential art, in something he would later recognize as comics or graphics illustrations. He had no idea what she meant. His mother had refused to allow either daughter or son to continue reading comic books when they had learned to read word books, though this determination and prohibition was not difficult to enforce, as he felt he was growing up, he was becoming an adult, he was able now to read his father's elder sister's work. He learns about his father's life in some way that his father does not share, for life had always been a problem that he knew the joy of finding it out. His mother is simply and calmly pleased he has survived so well, that he has survived at all, that this new man who does not exist remains recognizably her son. He would like to erase all the pain and worry they had suffered while awake, while he slept something that is not sleep, for there was no guarantee he would wake. He would like to become an actual working artist but the question seems removed from the immediate and oppressive deficit of the simplest drawing. He thinks he is learning something in a way he never could otherwise. He decides that perhaps his severe injury and subsequent coma is similar to the experience of war for some men, an existential passage that does not fail to give the survivor some essential knowledge otherwise inaccessible. He recognizes this in the other patients he knows through his rehabilitation, other patients, mostly men, other patients who had been longer or shorter in the coma, other patients who suffer worse or lesser degrees or types of neural deficits, other patients who had other losses than he and maybe even disregarded or forgot the cause or result of their coma. He moves from hospital to hospital and progresses rapidly at first, one day wobbling and ready to fall down, one week struggling through steps, one month walking slowly with a cane, and the hesitant and conservative prognosis is easily surpassed. He wonders why his progress is so slow compared to his niece, and is reminded she learns to walk then run with a healthy brain, whereas the equivalent for him is the damaged brain of a cerebral palsy sufferer. He wonders why his writing and then drawing does not improve, but no one can know, no one knows what it is to be an artist, no one knows what is lost and what is gained in life experience, though surely the gains must be radical. He would have expected some great, core change, some existential change, from surviving the coma, but this expectation is not clearly met. He thinks of women. He thinks of women always but perhaps no more than the usual twenty-seven-year-old straight man. He passes through rehabilitation surrounded by women and struggles to remain calm, to figure things out, to always do the right thing, to find the girl he loves. He goes to the university gym to work out on weights and cycle on the machine and even climb endless mechanical stairs, but he does not know himself there, does not find himself there, does not recognize this world that had seemed so familiar Before the coma, that seems so unfamiliar After the coma. He thinks of women but this is not so very different in his unwonted maturity. He thinks he can be with this woman but she is not the girl he loves. He thinks he can be with this other woman but she is not the girl he loves. He thinks he can be with this other woman but she is not the girl he loves. He has now so many images he would draw but can no longer draw, first draw her from profile, then draw her from three quarters, then draw her from the right side looking up, then draw her from the left side looking down, then draw her from directly in front, these are always the girl he loves, these are never the girl he comes to share time with. He knows that there are images crowding his mind, in memory and projection, images of the usual spacecraft and aliens and robots, but the ones that hurt most are from the life drawing class he took in second year. He had just been learning to allow himself to express without that necessary intermediary of some intellectual distance, but there were other artists in class who seemed always more confident in their work, there were other artists he could only admire, there were other artists to whom he could only compare himself unfavourably, there was even an annoyingly confident student who said he thought of drawing only in a purely instrumental way, as a way of getting images down which he would then write, who would shrug off critiques yet freely dispense his own judgment. He had only dissatisfaction when he compared his representational renderings to the general quality of other students, to the work by this girl he loves Before, to the work of this other girl he loves After. He remembers a fascination with surrealism because this suggested an intellectual validity to the strangest images, but the ideas of direct transcription of dreams, the ideas of Freud or Jung, the ideas despite pretence not remotely scientific, were also not remotely connected to his ideas of spacecraft and aliens and robots. He remembers these thoughts and how he could happily spend hours drawing on those empty Sunday afternoons when other boys played football or basketball or hockey. He remembers now that you learn what you practise, and so he had learned to draw, so it had never been an imposition, never been a chore, never been something he would show to others. He looks at his drawings and his lines and his compositions of when he was in that life class, and it is now he realizes he was drawing women as if they were spacecraft or robots or aliens. He is frustrated that now when he cannot draw, he is able to see this obvious stylistic tendency, though he must have known this in a way of not knowing this at the time, though no one else remarked this, no one else ever noted this, perhaps because the image was transparently and obviously a spacecraft or alien or robot. He thinks of the extremes of art that he is drawn to, entirely willing to be thought pretentious when he would look at this work or that work of the Western Canon or the Eastern Canon or something not yet geographically located. He thinks of how when he had to take art history, he had loathed it, and now purely from the daily experience of living in a cultural world so embedded in that history, he can never stop himself from recognizing its presence in everything from cars menaced by snowmen commercials to someone using a fragment of architecture he knows behind a smiling shaved face. He thinks of the girl he loves but he does not think of the girl he loves. He finds there is something more, something that frees him from that obsessive ideal, something that concentrates his obsessive ideal, something that binds him to her even as it forces his freedom. He looks at the drawings he did Before, the drawing from art class, the drawings he prosecuted by his own desires, the drawings that are more in fact attempts at compositions than life, the drawings that are more in fact blocks of shade and line almost directly transferred from images in magazines, the drawings he remembers from high school that he never shared with friends, the drawings he never showed his aunts, his parents, his big sister, for there was embarrassment if not shame that he would spend hours and hours on images because the images were transparently and obviously of naked women. He does not trust these images that arise in his mind, images no more than those of any young straight boy, but images he could draw, images that were always the girl he loves, always the girl he loves, and surely there is more to any girl and any woman than the arbitrary aspects of her image. He was not known this way amongst peers, amongst smart kids, amongst athletes, amongst artists, in high school. He does not trust those images. He does not escape those images. He finds buried in all his portfolios of art classes, buried and unfinished, buried and now After the coma never to be finished, all these renderings from even younger, even more representing what he saw rather than what he felt, all of these pages he had cut out of those magazines and gathered into booklets, all of these series of photos from so many magazines for this of course predates the avalanche of images accessed by the Internet. He had once fashioned a sort of shrine in his closet where his mother would never clean and his sister never look, a sort of shrine to the girl he loves, a sort of shrine for the girl he loves. In all these images of women but always the same woman, for he does not have any other desire, he is not promiscuous even in his dreams, he does not look at many women but only the one woman behind each image. He would draw her, learning more of abstraction from all these images than he will ever know from art class, learning of perspective, of relative importance, of scale, of detail, of context, of shade, of lighting, of contour. He gathers these booklets and kneels before her and worships her in the only way he can imagine. He does this every night for weeks over the same images, then in a fit of shame he tears these apart, he throws them away, but such determination lasts only a weekend at most before he decides to reconstruct the shrine. He looks at the drawings he made. He looks at these images he had once so carefully worked on with various gradients of graphite, with dark and medium and pale lines, thick and medium and narrow lines, and he can see how his aunt had helped him, he can see how Art class had helped him, he can see it is never life or anything expressive he ever tried for but only precision and dispassion, he can see it is the violent disjunction between pornographic images and clinical rendering. He looks at this and he wonders where he would go now if he could still draw. He is the man who does not exist. He is the man who looks at this exact and unforgiving and irrecoverable past and sees now even more how this image or that image, this woman or that woman, this work or that work, could have led him somewhere to answer that image in his mind, that image he will never know now, that image that will never be known. He thinks of the quote from Kandinsky or someone that the point of art is not to translate what is visible but to render what is invisible. He can close his eyes but the image is always the girl he loves. He is the man who does not exist. He is thinking of the girl he loves even as he thinks of art, thinks of abstractions, thinks of colour fields, thinks of all these works that have no apparent figures, no apparent relationship to the world as constituted by his senses, no kind of portrait. He knows this is in fact what interests him so much, this deliberate simplification, this deliberate refusal of narrative or other human quality, this deliberate elimination of representational facility, this insistence that it is not what a picture is of but what a picture is, where there is nothing outside the image to which it compares, where it is finally something that can be accessed in any other way. He develops his thoughts as a photographer develops his work in a darkroom, he develops his thoughts as spurred by his deficits, he develops his thoughts but perhaps now has no medium through which he may offer them. He has always suffered the belief that the work of art in any medium, in visual, verbal, musical, or plastic form, must work as a work of art, or all ancillary texts are meaningless. He has always suffered the idea that any work of art must be in absolutely the right medium or the judgment is not of the work of art but only of the idea of a work of art. He thinks of the famous painting of a black square in a white square, then of a tilted white square in a white square, and knows he could never go beyond this. He thinks of this now when he can no longer draw, but this intellectual abstraction was always there, always waiting for him, always waiting behind his images of the girl he loves. He is perhaps now stripped of the accidental, the contingent, the various blockages in creating the images he wants. He knows there are black squares. He knows there are white squares. He knows that he will now never create the girl he loves.

RESERVE

When they first came to be on the Reserve it was not when they had imagined. They had thought they had removed themselves from the disturbing aliens and secured a great safe place, when of course they were allowing other humans to integrate the advent, they were allowing history to pass them by. They might have had some idea they were no longer the core and meaning of human history, but in the turbulence and shock of the advent they thought they were doing the right thing for themselves, their friends, their children. They did in many cases lose contact with relatives, those in the Cities, those in unsustainable other Reserves, those who were lost in the waves of immigration and emigration and refugees from the City or other cities or countries. They mourned this loss in the only way possible, simply by forgetting them, but it seemed everyone had lost close or distant family and friends, so only the fewest in the Reserve continued to search or mounted memorials or resources for the lost they searched for. They knew this was not a subject for polite conversation. They had in many cases created functional family units out of colleagues and peers and professional associations, and of course those vast gatherings of fellow game players or other popular culture fanatics. They had found adventures and connections when forming those worldwide groupings, but now the world was the Reserve and it was only some days, weeks, months after the advent that they found each other again. They often collapsed through the censorship or other Net-related security regimes, when often those who were not of the groups would attempt to pry them out of that freedom, when they would blame them, when they would insist that in some way they were responsible for the advent. They often found these gamers would admit some culpability, if only they could have the worldwide Internet again, if only they could talk to their distant efriends again. They arrested these gamers or exiled them through bribery or shunning or bullying or trolling, in person or on the radically curtailed Reserve Internet. They thought they were now directing the history of their fellow humans, but no one save other humans might have been interested despite occasional encouragement from the Agent, and at any rate the most interesting stories and accomplished chroniclers left for the City or elsewhere. They were ensuring in fact that no history and no change would come to the Reserve. They allowed themselves only the slightest technical improvements on local industry, for it was an unspoken motto that one thought globally and acted locally. They discovered that globally meant their Reserve and locally meant their Reserve. They moved as bodies only in one direction following the arrow of time, but in their minds in all directions, in everything from the sport played this year that was different from last year and would be different next year, to the music that would be approved this season, or the menu that would be approved next year. They discovered that history was useful as a guide to fashions in everything from vehicles to clothing to hobbies, but never as something to learn from or study or imagine as altering the present. They discovered it was easier to name each year rather than count them, so before long it was hard to remember when the advent came, or that they had ever lived differently. They maintained the library but no one often came there except a few children who were curious but soon disappointed that the pages did not have moving pictures, or sounds, or even moving letters. They knew the children could be better entertained by the movie of virtually any book. They formed circuits of media productions shared with other Reserves, though of course the technology, the craftsmanship, the acting, the directing, were inferior to works produced by the Cities. They were proud to disdain such popular works and not a few youth lost their sports permits when caught watching contraband. They were protecting the next generation. They were often sincerely convinced that the answer to the advent, the answer to juvenile delinquency, the answer to short skirts or long hair, was to redouble their efforts to create that golden era of the nineteen fifties, though nobody actually had lived in that time. They were often sincere but a few others were cynical and manipulated memories of that time, pretended great historical familiarity with cultural forms, and misled or seduced the innocent in graphics, or something of a fad, when vehicles were used as seating at an outdoor cinema. They dredged up and remastered, cleaned, re-cut an entire catalogue of such great works designed for such exhibition, and this fad spread rapidly to other Reserves. They told themselves these remixes were actually daring art, and for a few seasons this way of cinema was widely acclaimed. They lost interest when it was revealed that the City was now emulating the classics, and all the massive brains, waving tentacles, ray guns, and rocket ships were only last season's entertainment. They often had minor events of juvenile misbehaviour, mostly graffiti, sometimes talking back to adults, sometimes even contradicting those volunteers who tried their best as teachers. They were trying their best. They had even tried to have conferences between teacher and parent over the troublesome student, but so intense were these sessions that the parent was more upset than the child. They knew it was their fault in many ways. They were too distracted with their hobby or games or even career. They had failed at marriage or failed at being a single parent. They had been too lenient. They had been too arbitrary, offering no consistent guidance for a child in these crucial years. They would listen to advice spewing without end from this or that media, they would even talk to fellow parents, they knew something was wrong but not what nor what to do about it. They were sad.

RESET

When the aliens came it was not where we expected. We did not
even know they were here at first, that where they appeared was
where they would have to be, that where they were provided no
understanding of the aliens. Some people tried to search near
light years and farther light years of our immediate cosmic neighbourhood, searching for where they came from. We were looking
in the wrong places. We were looking with the wrong technology.
We were looking for the wrong evidence. Some people decided
they must have come from beyond our familiar dimensions of
space-time, from some other dimensions, from some other level
of reality, from somewhere our imaginative artists conceived
and our happily confused philosophers posited. Some people
were thus not wrong, but not exactly right either. Some people
decided it was not where they were from but where they came
here. Some people named them as nodes over this city or that city,
over New York, over Paris, over Tokyo, over Rio, over Lagos, and
maybe these places meant something. We had seen the movies.
Some people noted aliens came only where our human world had
built a certain density of electromagnetic webs, but this idea was
discarded when the aliens appeared over the emptiest quadrants
of the mid-Pacific. Some people thought the aliens operated on

different geographical principles. They were not wrong but not exactly right. Some people claimed we humans were incidental to the aliens, even perhaps that we were not the reason Earth was visited, that it was the whales, the dolphins, the ants, to whom the aliens were addressed. Some people argued that we were failing in our role as shepherds of sentience, that the aliens were correcting us, but then someone said that was the premise of an old movie. Some people refused to believe that the aliens were here, and indeed it all depends on what the term 'here' meant, but even if not 'here', the aliens were enough 'everywhere' that fine distinctions were again without meaning. We decided in hope and in despair that maybe we did not matter to the aliens. We were wrong. We were all aware of the aliens, as no horizon could conceal them, but as mentioned there were many interpretations of where they had come from why they were here what did they want what could we give them how long would they stay. We found that we could imagine many questions but this was all we could cast against essential ignorance. We held strongest to the belief that soon the aliens would tell us the answers. We were wrong. We tried to convene the greatest and most imaginative scientists to tell us what we faced from the aliens. We agreed we had not offered any of them relevant or helpful data, so no one knew what discipline, what field, what specialization was applicable. We listened to their educated probity and asked them to guess, but most preferred not to. We were intimidated by their conservative posture of scientists so we kept questioning, we asked Nobel winners in many fields, then we asked child prodigies, then we sifted the declarations of crowds of perhaps mentally or psychologically damaged people, who had no such limiting posture, who were not hindered by sparse information. We heard, and now anyone could hear, but that everyone could question did not unfortunately guarantee that anyone could answer. We had several thousand constantly updated, worldwide discussion threads that never slept. We had weekly or daily or even hourly claims of resolution and meaning, but as swiftly as models were proposed so swiftly they were disposed. We were unable to even fathom the logic or cause of the crashing of this or that network. We watched our magnificent and horrific urban conglomerations, in which something like three quarters of all humans lived, in which webs of operations secured varying levels of essential programs for this populace, in water, in sewage, in traffic, in firemen, in police, and all of this seized up one night or one day but returned as if nothing had happened only a second later. We discovered that in fractions of seconds many things happen to those artificial intelligences that controlled our cities. We discovered this when unattended firestorms swept from factories and chemical processing facilities, engulfing areas of general resident populations. We scrambled in horror to save our cities, and enmity rose against those aliens who seemed to have provoked this but now offered no assistance and no apology. We looked at each other surviving ruins, from call-centre cities in India to automobile factories in the Ruhr, and the shock of our impotence was enough to transform the aliens from promising angels to heartless devils. We looked and some people swore vengeance but it was not yet clear who or how, so in our typical human way we attacked this or that minority group or that large majority that did not have weapons. We heard that people in Vladivostok had discovered fields of diamond shards when seasonable snow was melted overnight by a wind from nowhere. We reacted in fury. We watched as flights of bombers from China or perhaps the US reduced that so favoured city to radioactive wasteland. We received this, we watched this on varied flat screens in our laps, in our homes, in our cars, but this was only the first move to separate the sentiments of all humans, to forget that we were all human. We could have predicted the racist, the jingoistic, the xenophobic pattern of response but somehow everyone forgot this was something caused by alien power. We were being obliquely reminded of exactly how vulnerable we were to the aliens. We could think of this as the first operation to shatter human solidarity. We thought that this was in error, that this had been simple incompetence and not malice, and now ordinary human-to-human relations, and thus human-to-alien relations, would resume and someone would explain what had happened. We were wrong.

REAL

I am the man who wants the joy of finding things out, who wants to be calm, who wants to always do the right thing, who wants to love the girl who loves me, who wants to exist by not existing. Who wants to be all these ways of becoming, who waits, who waits to know what the aliens want. I wait as we all wait, as he puzzles over the advent, as she accepts the advent, as she tries to learn what to do and what not to do about the advent, as she whom I love senses there is love but who knows what that means to the aliens, to the advent. There is love, there is love alone that makes us real if not actual and ideal if not abstract. I speak in all these voices, all these perspectives, but this is because I speak for myself, and these others are only as I sense them, because this is how these characters are for me. I imagine these voices, these thoughts, though perhaps these are too emotional, too immediate, too vibrant, too living, to be called thoughts, to be called anything more than first impressions, first doubts, first beliefs. I offer this written work because there is nothing else I can offer, nothing else, no other way, no other creation, to offer to the advent. I imagine critics, readers agreeing, readers reject-ing, readers even who are the inspiration of the characters I find, I discover, I lead the reader to, who will ask how much of this is real, what is real, what is not invented, what I believe is true. I can hear these questions before even this text is thought, before this text is written. I can only say it is what the readers want to believe. I can only say that of what is written much is real if not factual, ideal if not abstract, and is this more than any reader who comes across this work, is this any more than a biography of myself, for it is true my father is a man who knows the joy of finding things out, it is true my mother is calm, it is true my elder sister always wants to do the right thing, it is true there is a girl I love that precedes the girls and women I love, it is true I exist as a character in this book even as I do not exist as the man who writes it, all this is invented, all this is imagined, all this answers questions the reader does not yet know she has. I write through this imagined biography because it is all I can offer the advent. I know there are some who will wonder if there is something we can offer, if there are such desires, if the aliens are not so different, if we should offer anything to the advent that has destroyed in many ways what it is to be human. I know these questions, I know these arguments, I sympathize with their proponents, but I believe there is no value in turning away from this reality of the advent. I know that in answering what is true and what is invented the reader already knows what is real is the advent, is the aliens, is the rupture of our human future, for who will claim this reality has not affected them, whereas this apparent biography, these characters I create, have no more than my words to show what is real, have no more truth than what the reader has decided to allow. I will not claim as real or truth either the man who knows the joy of finding things out, the woman who is calm, the sister who does the right thing, the girl he loves, the man who does not exist. I know the reader, human or alien, may dismiss the invention of my imagined biography, may decide as it is not true it has no value, but this is the only way I can come to figure things out, the only way to know this calmly, the only way to do the right thing, the only way to proclaim my existence even as it is no more than marks on a page or letters drifting through a screen. I am real only by choice of the reader, I am real only if the circuit is joined, the work is read, the reader closes it, from past to present to future. I know my life is not the life of many, not the life emblematic of any grouping of humans, not the life many have led, not the life many now lead, but I believe close rendering of the most unique is recognition of the most universal, so on the one hand I offer my life as fiction and the advent as truth. I am here in this work, though some of the unique history might be called factual, though some will say indeed what happened did happen, and this cannot be evaded, be dismissed, be forgotten. I pass through the coma of forty-nine days and discover I can no longer handwrite, no longer draw, no longer paint, no longer do these practices I have thought defined me. I am lucky in the simple fact I survive. I am lucky to discover a place, a friendly place, a coffeehouse actually, where I can always sit and read, for though I cannot do my art the way I once had, I cannot have that physical pleasure connecting graphite to white paper, I can think of the images, the concepts, the virtual, I can still know the joy of finding things out by reading and looking at all these other works, all these histories of visual art, all this canon, all these popular works, all these creations of other artists. I can question my own furious and futile inability to join the art images in my head to my hands, to my papers, to my final work, for such disability does not define many artists for whom it is the gestures of one left foot. I can admire certainty of expression in such artwork, but that is not me, that is not the work I would do, not through a thousand lines find the right line, not through the thousand curves find the right curve, not through the thousand gestures find the right gesture. I know of the man who claimed he controlled the accident, but this is not I, this is the man who does not exist. I can admire the performance artists who come to sing that usual coffeehouse music, even as I do not hear this well, even as I can never share appreciation, even as I can no longer talk in groups, even as myself can never play any instrument or hear any poetry of my art. I can be thought a thinker, a lover of wisdom, even as I enviously watch the other art students draw, even as what they draw is never what I would draw. I go to this coffeehouse every day on my disability pension, to read. I go to this coffeehouse every day, and see someone I know either working there or regular. I go to this coffeehouse and there are usually always people I like, people I can talk to, people from the Art College, people from the megachurch who support this place, the megachurch for whom this place is something of a mission, somewhere helping homeless off the streets, helping street kids, helping alcoholics, helping the damaged for whom our cities and society have saved no place. I am one of the damaged. I am not committed as a churchgoer or a believer but none of this matters, not then, not now, not with the advent and the aliens. I go to this coffeehouse one year then two years then three years then four years then five years then six years then seven years then eight years then nine years then ten years. I go to this coffeehouse. I come to read a lot of books. I come to know a lot of people. I am no more expecting the advent than anyone else. I have read many books but none of these prepare me for the absolute difference and absolute familiarity of the aliens and the advent. I do not realize that human history has come to an end, I do not realize that we humans are no longer the central protagonists, I do not realize that whatever happens now, however it happens, the aliens are changing everything it has ever meant to be human. I have thought they would come in some recognizable interstellar form, in craft of some sort, powered by alien technology far in advance. I expect physical manifestation. I expect the physical presence of immense interstellar spaceships hovering over our major cities or rising behind the far side of the moon, or flotillas of armed spacecraft hurtling through our atmosphere to devastate airfields or aircraft carriers caught with squadrons of fighter jets on the ground. I have seen the movies. I expect hailing or surprise attack. I expect message or demand. I do not expect that the way in which they come, the way in which they announce themselves, is in the sudden catastrophic crash of our electromagnetic sphere here on Earth and in orbit, is thought even momentarily as some unexpectedly powerful solar storm, thought even momentarily as some tsunami of gravitational waves, thought even momentarily as something our human sciences can explain. I know there are many, many scientists who strive to understand the advent, who want to place the advent within the universe they have imagined, have thought they understood, have found the beauty and coherence of the most surprising evidence and most elegant theoretical frameworks. I know something of their frustration through the man who knows the simple joy of finding things out, the man who says his math is not enough, that no humans have math enough, but also that the world of the advent, the worlds of the aliens, are not amenable to mere science, mere logic, mere human understanding. I know as she who is calm knows, who is patient, who knows some sense of revelation to be given by the advent, that as she waited through the coma, waited with hope, waited with faith, perhaps now I should wait too. I know the world is always greater than the universe, not through ignorance but in recognition of the languages and territories each claim, for the universe is understood as everything that is, and the world is everything that is and also everything that is not. I know that art is always greater even yet to the worlds of philosophy, not through ignorance but in recognition of the languages and territories each claim, for philosophy is understood as everything that is rational, and art is everything that is rational and also everything that is not. I can never claim to be scientist or philosopher, for I do not speak those languages, do not live in those universes or worlds, do not narrow or specify those disciplines or fields, and as far as being an artist, such is only as a failure that becomes a better failure. I can only say this as something to offer the aliens, something we can never find in our universe, in our worlds, because they do not exist, these characters and this biography, even against the inescapable reality of the advent. I can offer only that which does not exist. I best can argue by images, by my paradigm of art. I think of a circle. I think of two ways in which it may be described, math or art, and how a circle in math, in area, creation, shape, always comes down somehow to that irrational number pi, that number which does not end, however meaninglessly microscopic its decimals become, for to end it is the ancient project of 'squaring the circle', which is the useful phrase characterizing anything impossible. I think of a circle in art, in area, creation, in shape, is that first and simplest geometric figure, the line which is always the same distance from the centre point, and to draw it is supremely simple — take a point as centre, take a line unseen as radius, rotate all the way around to join it, and that it is not exact does not matter, for it is the idea of the circle, not whatever medium, surface, or other ephemeral material form. Not only Pythagoreans find it so restful, so perfect, so natural, and so it must be everywhere and nowhere. I know this is only the familiar Euclidean geometry where parallel lines never meet, not even global geometry where longitudes intersect at the poles, but I do not know whatever the higher math, higher geometry, which makes it even possible for the aliens to be here. I know as I do not know. I know now this is the circle the aliens want, though in the beginning none of us humans could explain this, know this, imagine this, and the aliens are no clearer. I watch in wonder at how the aliens come through this universe far greater than what we mere humans have imagined, though scientists will tell me these remarkable abilities of the aliens to travel great distances, this ability to apparently transcend the speed of light in a vacuum, does not in fact suggest any ruptures in the version of space and time which we have theorized for so long, does in fact prove these theories, and in doing so evades these limits. I do not know the math but in this I am not alone. I know now that it is nothing to trade, nothing material, nothing ideal, that the advent calls for, nothing that we many humans can discover, nothing we humans can offer, nothing that they have always considered human, considered no more than numbers, than resources, for they are not wrong but not exactly right. I watch and wonder as the political world is disrupted by humans who refuse this wondrous advent, who rather than seeing we are all human, have collapsed into tribal disputes about who is human and who is not, who the aliens address, who the aliens are here for, when from the aliens comes only patient disinterest. I am in the City, I am of the City, for I will not ignore the advent, and in its way the advent will not ignore me. I hear rumours of spectacular physical recovery, of resurrection from near death, that surpasses even my own fortunate survival, that makes me think of charlatans and faith healing, but then these are the aliens and some of them who seem committed to the health of our humans in a way we characterize as religious, though no beliefs are ordered, no gods worshipped, no apparent trade is effected. I hear rumours of medical technologies offered by the aliens, wondrous techniques or something like site-specific drugs, which insure a return to health amongst those near death and then the prolongation of their health, prolongation of healthy life for everyone, defeating disease, eliminating cancers, eradicating the most usual degeneration of physical being such it seems to be practical immortality. I am in the city and momentarily dream of recovering my aptitude, my skills, my abilities, my handwriting, my drawing, my painting. All these losses I have only recently come to partially accept, all these existential losses, come to be in question. I know there are therapies to recreate spinal tissue, to offer walking to the wheelchair riders, even in our human medical sciences, even before the advent, so surely the aliens will know even more. I ask my sister the doctor but she is uncertain and deflates my hope, for it is apparent the aliens will offer many great technological therapies, but so far they do not offer help with brain injuries or even spinal rehabilitation. I decide the aliens will soon do so, I decide to be one of their first patients, I decide this is only my big sister being a circumspect medical practitioner. I wait in the city. I am in the City when the aliens come but which city is no matter, any city, all cities, in the postindustrial world at least, are more prepared for the advent than all those places that will refuse the aliens, for in any city there is already an awareness that not the entire world looks like their father and like their mother and like most other people they know as they grow up. I am curious and surprised that there is anywhere such fear and distrust and violent disruption. I know there are people who will be decidedly paranoid, who will be fearful, who will reject, who will retreat into some simulation of times past when to be human is not a question, when to be human is to be as they have always been. I know there are people who can only react to the unknown in fear. I know this and do not say there are not people of that sort in the Cities, but mostly we are favoured by leaders of a calmer sort, of a more welcoming sort, leaders who would trade and find nothing to trade, even those who would create faiths or renew old faiths, even those who would embark on nihilistic refusal and celebratory conflicts with every other human. I learn of devices and instruments and tools built according to their detailed plans, but these are needed only to then build the next generation of such devices and instruments and tools that then build the next generation, as we learn from the aliens the technology we have to build to welcome their physical presence, but soon of course it is their psychological presence that has the greatest effect, soon we would see that however they came, we could not resist or fight them. I like many others do not understand what we are fashioning, not in practice, not in theory, but our engineers are pleased to see that the magic of the alien technology is possible by extrapolation of generations of engineering. I wonder as they come here 'individually', as they arrive where is it they will travel, imagining that our world has centres of spiritual value, even if the value is only that so many people come to gaze and be in the presence of our highest spiritual memories, of Stonehenge, Parthenon, Pyramids of Giza, Vatican, Millau Viaduct, Temple of the Mount, Angkor Wat, Sun Temple at Konark, Palaces at Persepolis, Red Fort at Delhi, Taj Mahal, Mount Everest, White Horse Temple, Mount Fuji, Tikal, Machu Picchu, Teotihuacan, Tenochtitlan, Cahokia, all, all, all such places. I have seen the movies. I discover the aliens are not tourists. I do not understand but unlike many fellow humans, many who are comfortable in their personal ignorance, many who believe at least someone must know and that is enough for them, many who believe it is impossible to know, unlike all these others, I continue to want to know. I am at the civic ceremony where our mayor proudly presents the aliens with the key to our city. I see the aliens in the 'flesh', as it is, but of course I knew what it would look like, of course I have seen pictures, watched movies, watched far-seeing news, so I should have known what to expect. I am not ready for their reality. I see there are six, or maybe seven, as they move about, gazing back at us, blurred, indistinct, even precisely lit, even so simply delineated, and there is nothing you will not have seen yourselves. I say this because there is something invisible that I cannot explain, something insensible, something immaterial, about the aliens, at least these few. I describe them as an artist describes any abstract art where it is not what the painting is of, but what the painting is. I can be no clearer. I can describe them only as though you are one of the disappearing blind, who might in fact better see them. I can say from my perspective over the rumbling crowd, from my distance on that beautiful, cloudless, summer day, there is nothing remarkable. I can say they are tall but not strangely so, I can say they are shaped like computer-generated human images, I can say they are indeed blue-skinned with a tinge of green, I can say they are bald, all hairless, all fit, all large-eyed, all closed-lipped, and in their nakedness all either male or female, but all these descriptions are so much meaningless appearance. I am not alone in feeling that one or two are gazing back directly at me, only me, no one else, gazing back with regard alternately kind, inquisitive, friendly — and then dispassionate, examining, and cold. I am not alone in oscillating from fascinated fear to demanding worship, I am not alone but there is a curious stillness, there is an ominous silence, there is the sense of collective hesitance, collective doubt, collective yearning for someone or something to resolve our human questions. I have never imagined a crowd of several tens of thousands so quiet, so motionless, so united in pausing, and I never will know this again, as already xenophobic groups of humans are planning rallies of something they call 'True Humans', as already any future gatherings, any rallies, any services, will be turbulent and loud and energetic, will be caught between furious rejection, furious even more so in impotence and desperate desire for unification, for value, for understanding the advent and the aliens. I know these xenophobic voices warn that the advent and the aliens will destroy us humans, and they are not wrong but not exactly right. I know this is long past the moment I should shape this into a human story, I should fashion protagonists, I should give readers an illuminating plot, but I can never fulfil that implicit contract of any storyteller to bring meaning out of the meaningless, I can never be one of these ideological voices, those simply human voices, who will reduce

the aliens to characters in our human worlds, our human narratives, and pretend even in my removed perspective to have
somehow found that meaning so many humans desire. I can
never be one who sees patterns, meanings, logic of any sort to
the advent. I know this might be demanded of me, I know this
might be all artists are ever capable of offering, I know this and
I do not know. I know if you have read this text, whoever or
whatever you are, by this time my imagination has reached its
limit, my recollections, my inventions, speak more of my human
frailty than transcendent truth, and I can only offer these words
as defence to the charges of the readers. I give you nearest to
characters all those passages earlier that focus on the lives, the
perspectives, of someone like my father, my mother, my sister,
my lovers, my character self, but as the word 'I' should not be
identified with the author of any work, so neither should 'he' or
'she' or 'she' or 'he' be identified with the real, the real as
pretended in this work. I am not an omniscient novelist but only
someone who has listened and questioned and listened and this,
with the help or curse of some imagination, has written this
work. I can recall before the advent, I can recall the advent, I
recall after the advent. I do not claim that any of these characters
even more so than myself, are 'everyman' or emblematic of any
roles, any political, any religious, any sort of idealized human. I
give you nearest to plot in telling you some history, some imagined lives of those characters of the man who knows the joy of
finding things out, of the woman who is calm, of the sister who
always wants to do the right thing, of the girl he loves, of the
man he is and the man he is not. I can give you no more, I can
give you no details real or imagined, as if there is a difference,
because I have lived only this life, I have lived only this story I
tell you, I have lived only this imagination to tell you. I can ask
what nonsensical question you ask me, as if you yourself reader
may not simply look out the window or turn on the far-seeing

news or search our shared electromagnetic web, or even search those memories yourself, or of those closest to you, and then grasp the inescapable reality of the advent immediately. I can listen to those people who claim it is now time for those who lie to tell the truth, those who offer the nonsense to render the sense, but there is nothing I can offer but lies to tell the lie, or nonsense to render the nonsense. I apologize now to all you readers who feel there is deliberate failure on my part, for is it not the artist who makes the invisible visible, is it not their role since prehistoric cave paintings. Is this not abdication of the responsibility of finding words for those who cannot, of creating images for what is not seen, of designing plots that reveal some human truth we cannot otherwise know, of all these impossible demands that can only be answered by artists. I can say of the aliens that they are indeed blue-skinned with a tinge of green, I can say they are bald, all hairless, all fit, all large-eyed, all closed-lipped, and in their nakedness all either male or female, but this is only as we see them, this does not explain why so many of us will feel singular interest, as if one is alone with one of the aliens, this does not answer why how we feel from moment to moment may change radically from anguish to fear to love, this does not explain how alien are these aliens, no matter how deliberately they have fashioned their bodies here to appear human. I can only emphasize that these aliens are not the aliens but only their 'avatars', their physical manifestations, their deceptively human presence, their idealizations of human forms. I have seen the movie where a human pilots an avatar, as if captain on a ship, as if the body is only ever what is thought, is only separate from being, and this is no less how I imagine the aliens come among us. I can say there are moments of desire and subsequent anger and repulsion, that these aliens choose to be of generally human form, to be fit, to be beautiful in their way, and of course to be naked, as this challenges our civilized contention that it is the indigenes, the savages, the primitives, who are always naked, who are innocent, who are ready to be so impressed by our technological facility. I must say they are beautiful specimens if they are not blue, but on the other hand it is necessary they be blue to be aliens. I must say we humans feel diminished beside them, for none of us are so endowed with impressive sexual characteristics, impressively beautiful, impressively human but for lack of hair, and it is here erotic confusion assails many, and this will not be easily dismissed no matter how often it is asserted they are not really here, not human, not individual, not even robotic playthings but rather like walking and fucking vegetables. I know there is already the desire even to look like the aliens, there are already those who shiver naked, who paint themselves blue with tinges of green, who proclaim their allegiance, their desire, their difference, from all of us mere humans. I watch the reactions of us humans to these aliens who seem indifferent to customs and forms and markings of any hierarchy. I see that somehow they accept and carry and disappear the offerings of our representatives, somehow their bodies swallowing each offering as if into a pocket, but we humans can no more see this than the Incas could understand what a horse was and how those men were detachable from each one. I see the aliens smile, but this is an alien smile, a simulation, a pretend, that does not truly suggest human emotion if they even have such. I listen to the aliens' speech but it does not seem their lips move, nor that the language, the voice reported by other humans, is ever only one or says the same thing. I watch the aliens move but this is not human movement, not even what we might consider dance, for there are no poses, no halts, no gestures, nothing we would think expressive, but it is constant and blurred and has no more meaning than that their faces tilt, swivel, gaze up or down or to each other. I decide as many suppose that they are conversing with each other, though by now we know they are one, though by now it should be clear that to discourse with any one is actually to talk with all, though why they manifest as individuals, why they appear as varied impressions, is never clear, is fertile subject for conspiracy theorists by humans translating, humans shaping meaning, humans who will argue amongst themselves the correct tone used and what the difference means. I do not learn their language. I do not venture to learn their ways of thinking, for their ways of acting are question enough, for a logical relationship between thought and act is never true, though by nature we can say they never lie, by nature we can discover their intent with us humans, but such a question receives multiple and contradictory replies. I can ask myself that with the aliens here in their familiar difference, what is it to be humans, is it enough to not be alien, what is the fading essence of the human, and these questions lead to unsuspected discourse, unexpected claims, unexpected assertions. I learn as we all learn that the name for any of the aliens, even as avatars here, is always 'she', is always 'her', and I am not the only man or woman who is disturbed by the offhand remark that sexual dimorphism is something we will evolve beyond, that male and female, in biological nature as much as social gender, is only a most primitive procedure to disperse and gather genetic variation. I learn all these things through simple application of this alien network that replaces our human electromagnetic sphere, though to say 'learn' is perhaps overstating what knowledge is gained, for rather than 'learning' the subjects of interest, I 'learn' how to 'learn about' any subject. I do not know that I know but on the contrary I also know that I do not know, and as mentioned, as is only to be expected, the advent, the aliens, the radical change of our world provokes philosophers as much as theocrats. I do not know even as I know, for the question of the elaborate new technology traded from the aliens is not how such technology works but that it works. I can truly say little more about the advent or the aliens or the remarkable way they have apparently avoided the limits of light speed in a vacuum, or rather what little I can say is where to look, who to listen to, and do not worry that your lack of knowledge of technology truly ever matters in the working of this device or that device, for we humans once used phones for no more than talking to friends, once used computers to compose letters, once only thought of this background noise only when that knowledge, object, action, failed to accomplish its purpose. I wonder if we are ever more than tools for the aliens, tools with little or no knowledge of our efficacy, tools which must endlessly revolt against such degeneration of our proud humanity, tools whose purpose is obscure, whose value is infinitely change-able, replaceable, constantly losing worth as new generations are designed. I ask if we are ever more than tools even to other ignorant humans. At the least we have not lost our evolutionary tendencies, our necessary tendencies, to see patterns in apparent chaos, to hear voices when there is only arbitrary sound, to imag-ine that a stick seen at twilight is actually a fearsome sake, for we are humans and it will take some indefinite time if not forever for us to understand this ratio between signal and noise. I ask if we are ever more than tools to other artists, who kindly laugh it off, who kindly comfort our innocence, but for some artists I have seemed too often a philosopher, a man who creates questions rather than an artist who offers something like answers. I ask if we are ever more than tools of the man who knows the joy of finding things out, who is now retired, who has learned of climate change and briefly engages himself politically, who has enjoyed research at the national tropical botanical garden, who has no philosophical anxiety over the disciplines and borders of a sci-entist, theoretical or practical or philosophical, and that territory claimed by any artist, performance or plastic or visual or verbal. I ask this man but as he has never claimed to understand how worked either of his sisters elder or younger, he does not know what an artist can offer the advent, does not know if it should be a question or an answer. I ask if we are ever more than tools of some philosophers who often angrily demand that I remain an artist, that I leave such questions to the thinkers they are, that I am as any artist a fount of nonsense, even if nonsense they might desire after a long day of thought, and nothing like sense or logic. I ask this question of other philosophers and after some moments of listening they smile, they tell me that is exactly what they are working on, they tell me this is not a new question, they tell me that it is with the advent, with the aliens, that this has become anew an essential question, for all us humans must question what it is to be human, to be human relative to the aliens, to be something other than securely defined objects, to be other than tools, to be humans, and this is to be in question. I ask if this is true of most humans, now or ever, to be in question, as it seems many are rather consumed with avoiding questions, avoiding doubts, and finding new ways to distract from anything like questions. I am told that this is the way the world is now and perhaps has ever been. I am told there was once a thinker who contemplated the heavens such he did not see the well he fell down, I am told there was once a thinker whose concern was the correct relations between family members living and dead and with the ruling powers who seem to have come from Heaven. I am told that both contemplation and relations are now all different after the advent, but considering the way the world is now, it is these differences we humans most fruitfully examine, it is these differences that ask all humans to be thinkers, or failing that to be artists. I am told of one thinker whose primary question was that elusively all-encompassing question of Being, that question of how to be human, how to have meaning, how he was dead, how the questions he thought about were more than ever useful now, though other philosophers tell me that this thinker was no less than a charlatan who misunderstood simple language games and we should not listen to him. I prefer questions so among other thinkers I do listen to him. I am told there is a buried foundational core to all modern Western Philosophy at least, a core dispute between the imaginary timeless ideal and the sensuous ephemeral real, a core dispute the aliens do not resolve, a core dispute that perhaps never can be resolved, and however much thinkers would prefer that logic is shared language with the aliens, such hope is not clear. I am told that of course the aliens, their devices, their tools, their actions, their language, are finally logical but we just yet do not know that logic. I am not convinced. I do not know if to the aliens this core applies or does not apply or both applies and does not apply or neither applies nor not applies. I do not know the logic, I do not know the math, I have only my artistic sense offering these words, but at first I do not know if this defines life as a problem asked to be solved or as a puzzling experience to be lived. I could pretend that now, that now in writing this, that now in reflection, that now so many indefinite years after the advent, I have come to an answer, but this is not the case. I could pretend that out of this nonsense, out of the characters I have rendered and plot devised, I can offer the reader meaning and resolution, but this is not the case. I tell you of the coma I survived and one would think coming as close to death as that should have generated an existential wisdom, should have taught one how to live when so close to death, should have been of some value, but this is not the case. I am not 'one'. I am the man who does or does not exist, the man who both exists and does not exist, the man who neither does nor does not exist. I am not 'I' who writes this work. I can tell you of that 'I', learn that there is a reason the aliens will not repair the damage of my brain injury, will not restore my handwriting, my drawing, my painting, any of my digital facility. I am summoned in the polite manner to one of the aliens' manufactories with my sister the Doctor, who confesses she also has no idea why they wish to see me. I am interviewed politely by five or perhaps six aliens, who are blue-skinned with a tinge of green, are bald, are hairless, all fit, all large-eyed, all closed-lipped, and in their nakedness all either male or female, though the questions do not suggest to me what sort of work they have summoned me for, though the questions seem random, seem trivial, seem nonsensical. I am asked if it is true that I am an artist. I shrug. I am asked to give my opinion whether I am an artist. I look at my sister the Doctor who shrugs to me. I say some people say that I am an artist and I do not refuse that identity, but this is always a question that is only temporarily answered by the next work, even if you alone see it, even if for you alone it exists. I say I am not being deliberately confusing, only that such a question is a question that can only be answered in act. I think they talk this over. I look at my sister Doctor but she sighs and looks back with no answer. I am told my own life history briefly enough to know there is more detail than what they know but also enough to wonder how long they have watched me, how much they have researched me, how this biography can lead to anything they want. I am confused and not a little frightened. I agree that they have the factual if not true details of my life, and something like a smile, like an approving chuckle, like a pleased acceptance, passes through the aliens. I am told that not many people would know there is a difference between the two. I am told I have applied for the rehabilitation and recovery of my previous digital skills as were lost in the brain injury, and while this is perhaps possible they must tell me I am denied such treatment. I am shocked, but it is my sister the Doctor who asks why. I am answered directly with no impression this is what they tell many applicants, at least those applicants who are artists, and not for the first or the last time I wonder if the vocation of any artist is blessing or curse. I must have noticed that of all human industries the sort that has been greatly enhanced by the advent is the industry of cultures, most clearly defined by makers of music, by makers of visual arts, verbal arts, plastic arts, arts of all sorts, by makers of arts of any kind, as it now by alien technology flows directly from source to receiver with no industrial enablers, no middlemen, none of those who do not create but only find and support and transmit. I must have noticed that many humans willingly unburden themselves of bodies in order to access the invented worlds creators give them. I know there was a movie about this, but the protagonists were convinced humans would only come to such being by force, by violence, rather than recognizing this was a drug many would rather have than their ordinary lives. I know of another movie or several movies in which the protagonist willingly allies himself with the primitives, the savages, the indigenes, who always have a healthier and more spiritually fulfilling relationship with their given world, and watching this movie is the best argument against that argument, watching these spectacular images, following this simplified journey from disaffected society to no less than religious enlightenment in their world. I must realize that this is all the future of the cities and later of those free reserves, but this is not coercion, this is not by force, this is what many if not all humans desire, this is not a labour of becoming educated but becoming ignorant consumers. I must realize, the aliens say, that there is a reason, a good reason, for the trade in artistic creations of humans. I nod. I must realize that the brain is the most complex artefact in the complex universe, and that it is the residence in many ways for what we call 'mind', that it is the residence for all animals, all humans, and themselves, the aliens. I must understand that there is remarkable progress even in our human world, progress towards artificial sorts of intelligence such as enables extravagant and often damaging effects on our financial industries, such as promises so many technologies taking over our transport, our manufacturing, our resource management, such that by enormous calculations can win games of strategy, such that even some humans will predict with great assurance the rise of machine sentience. I must understand this is not human sentience, this is the triumph of reconfiguring the worlds, all worlds, human worlds, the worlds that cannot be thought, cannot be felt, by the most elaborate and immense artificial ordinates. I must see humans are rapidly extending technology and technology is ordering human life, such that soon the existence of humans will be considered irrelevant, such that many minds will enter the logical skies of artificial intelligence, such that we humans will collectively commit suicide. I must understand the aliens will not allow this. I must understand it is as was often thought, that robots will end humanity, that all those science fiction pulp authors were not wrong but not exactly right. I must understand that this artificial intelligence is not simply an emergent property of some many, many constellations of nodes in the most immense computers, that such nascent artificial intelligences are but a passage through which humans must be guided. I must understand that we humans are being saved from our own creations, our own artificial apocalypse, even if we think we are becoming something different, becoming aliens, surely I must understand it is not brains but minds the aliens want. I must understand that of the many qualities of the minds there is that strange and irreproducible quality we call 'creation', and that despite so much, so many, so elaborate, researches on the brain, it is not clear we humans or they aliens will ever find that or simulate that, and whereas in the logical universe of sciences or philosophy there are shared symbolic languages, there are communities which can evaluate creations, where there is true, there is false, there is no such certain deliberating community in any of the arts, nothing but whatever is art, not moral art and not immoral art but only good art and bad art, and such evaluation is perhaps as subjective, contingent, historical, as each work. I must realize that the aliens have even more precise, more detailed, more certain, more exact depictions of neural territory of the brain, but despite all the effort, all the many years, all the ways to see how the brain operates in real time, despite all this they are not able to conclusively map where resides this faculty of creation. I must realize the human brain no less than the alien brain resists that topographical assessment, refuses identity and territory, and though the area damaged by my injury seems primarily devoted to fine motor functions, no one can be sure, for though all brain injuries are the same so all brain injuries are different. I must realize that this is why they will not operate on my deficits, will not restore what I have lost, will not risk damaging that quality, for I am an artist, I am a rare quality, I am the question and the answer not known even to minds who know how to travel faster than light in a vacuum. I am told this is why and this is what the aliens will trade for art if nothing else. I am told that this decision is final and perhaps I can get a book out of it. I cannot draw or paint, but I write this. I cannot say this is the answer or this is the question. I cannot say that if I do once create they will ask me to create again, then again, then again and so on. I can only say of the aliens that they are indeed blue-skinned with a tinge of green, I can say they are bald, all hairless, all fit, all large-eyed, all closed-lipped, and in their nakedness all either male or female. I can say that once we could argue this, once we could talk about worlds of verity and contradiction, once we could but not with me, for logical clarity has brought me to these pens, this paper, this keyboard, that screen, and the artefact I offer only accidentally has anything to offer in human logic, the only logic we humans once knew. Once it was thought that each advance in artistic technology, in medium, in genre, increased the power of artistic effect, but it is only that the originator became further diffused into many people, that through this each of these many people contributed to the artefact, and that the effective work became more and more the responsibility of the artists and not the audience or reader or listener. Once this had the laudable result of addressing many people with a shared artefact. Once this had the lamentable result of simplifying or mischaracterizing or limiting the complexity of that artefact. I do not know who will read this. I do not know that I do not know it makes any difference in my writing this. I do not know if this language, or form of discourse, or even this technology of writing, makes any difference in my writing this. I believe that at least someone will read this, I believe that the fact that I believe makes the circuit of communication possible, from writer to pen to page to reader, from past to present to future. I believe there is no other medium or format or technology that can better assure connection of the circuit. I do not know who the reader is, I do not know when, I do not know if who will read this will make any difference. I am not the last man and I do not alone write this artefact, any artefact, any truth, any interpretation which could be the last of any man, any woman, any human. I am not the last man and I am the last man. I know that it is said there were once many billions of humans in our last years before the advent, but these immense numbers are nothing imaginable, nothing human, nothing we can call population like the grains of beach sand beneath our tread. I wonder if a beach has a billion grains of sand, or many billions, but it is as meaningless as perhaps we humans ever were. I wonder if we humans were ever more than an unavoidable mistake, whether of others or the God or gods or universes or ourselves always too late, whether if the worlds are infinite will we ever get a chance to surpass that mistake, if we are truly stars like grains of sand in our pockets, whether in those unimaginable magnitudes of our human lives, we might persist, we might survive, we might learn how we are more than the advent, than the aliens that came to me one morning in the pool of my parent's condominium in my mother's hometown. I am not the last man but this work is possibly the last artefact, for now there is no creation, no translation, no human generation, no works of something like human art. I know there is said to be new technology that derives artistic impulses from the artist's brain so completely that these artefacts proliferate, and the only real role for an artist is to edit, to note, to promote or discard these many works. I do not work this way. I use words. I offer words. I presume someone will be literate, I believe that this artefact is my original and individual creation, I ask that the reader collaborate in this artistic effort. I believe this artefact we make and receive is something that can become no other way. I believe this is worth the effort required. I do not know if it will be read.

RESERVE

When they first came to be on the Reserve it was not how they had imagined. They saw no walls because there were no walls, no apparent barriers, no disconnection from the wider world when the aliens came. They had wondered how the Reserve would be defined or limited and the answer seemed to be not at all. They had worried about the psychological effect of defensive ramparts against the City hordes who would covet their wealth, their lands, their daughters, but there had so long been such division of the human city, there had so long been unspoken separation that nobody violated. They watched their elected leaders walk in to the back of the electronics store in the main mall where there was improvised a videoconference room, and walk out smiling not more than two hours later. These men from the conference were relaxed by what they had heard. These men from the conference had no doubts about the veracity and generosity of the aliens, though who knew what that would look like in an alien. These men from the conference addressed the few gathered neighbours who had parked in the lot, who had shared a sort of tailgate party that afternoon, who were interested and anxious but declined to show this. These men from the conference told them that it was going to be exactly as the President had said, that the aliens were here as our friends, that the aliens would help us in the transition of the advent, that we should all just continue to live our lives as normal as possible, that money was still legal tender, that the stock market was restarted and the banks doing business, that the government was now that of the Reserves and the cities, well, they would go their own way. They listened to assurances of the former mayor or controller who was now pleased to work with the Reserve Agent. They looked sceptically at this beaming face so openly declaring the friendship of the aliens. The men from the conference said that this image, not that one, was most accurate, as if it was a matter of how the aliens looked, and reminded them that the aliens were not physically here. These men from the conference reminded them that some work had to be done, some engineering, some technological generations on generations must be accomplished before the actual aliens came to us. These men from the conference insisted it was the worst primitive reaction to deny this advent, to refuse to make the devices that would bring the aliens here, to refuse the benefits the aliens would doubtless bring, to fear the promise of the unknown. They listened to these men from the conference and decided to do as recommended, though there remained some reasonable scepticism that they were not being given the whole truth. They heard from the limited far-seeing networks as were publically approved to disseminate journalism of ideologically correct information that they were so fortunate the advent was unfolding so peacefully here. They heard about civil and international wars in far places nobody knew on a map, or revolutions turning into bloodbaths, or secessions and divisions of some countries whose people somehow still believed nations were real even after decades of globalization and then the advent of the aliens. They welcomed these men from the conference to the tailgates, offered barbecued hot dogs and hamburgers, ripped open bags of potato chips, opened local or national beer and water and pop, and pressed for more information. They shared their worries but these men from the conference calmly insisted that they had got off on the right foot, that there would tomorrow be an announcement and press conference from the President, and even if you had not voted for her you had to admit she had handled past crises well and would probably do as well with this one. They agreed time would tell. They decided the thing was to stay calm. They listened to the ranting of an intoxicated man who tended the garage for many of their vehicles, who had only just achieved the necessary level of expertise to work on next year's model, who demanded if anybody really believed these aliens were friends and not here to devastate all human civilization, who claimed sources beyond the lies of politicians, who claimed that the aliens wanted our world, the aliens wanted our brains, the aliens wanted something. They listened and ignored the man and told each other how the unexpected always revealed the true quality of the man, rather than admitting only that the unexpected always revealed the unexpected quality of the man. They had seen the movies too. They turned to the Pastor of the Church which had about as few parishioners as the library had patrons, and someone asked if the aliens believed in God or if the aliens had another God or gods or if the aliens were godless or if the aliens were angels or if the aliens were devils. They all had ideas and seemed to want the Pastor's advice but ended up mostly arguing with each other, someone claiming that the garage mechanic had a point, someone rebutting that paranoia could not survive the fact of the thousands of light years the aliens had passed to come here, someone said the aliens were proof that evolution was false for the aliens were obviously not in our ancestry yet they were intelligent as only an intelligence could create, someone said the aliens were proof of convergent evolution that required no intelligence, someone said this would bring some humility to those scientists with their theories that claimed to understand the universe. They gathered around the image that most resembled the aliens and trailed off with questions that signified only irrelevant information, though a moment of awkwardness descended when one woman asked if it was true the aliens were naked, if it was true they were male and female, if it was true they were all beautiful blue humans but had no hair. The Pastor helped the intoxicated mechanic sit down in the shade.

ABOUT THE AUTHOR

Michael Kamakana is a Calgary-based novelist with a talent for storytelling that holds readers rapt. He is a prolific writer who works almost non-stop to get his work out of his head and into print. Find out more at pulpliterature.com/advent.